HIS WRATH

DEMON'S SIN BOOK 1

AVA HUSH

CONTENTS

CONTENT WARNINGS

- Mention of cheating, historic
- Mention of death of parent - violent, historic
- Rough sexual play and some sexual experimentation, all consensual.
- Hint of BDSM components/ references
- Mention of possible sexual assault
- Descriptions of torture and abuse
- Abstract religious ideologies

This book is intended for Adult (18+) readers.

CHARACTERS

Aridam - wrath demon, mate of Rhys
Rhys - partial null, mate of Aridam
Azvameth - sloth demon
Devland - greed demon
Kek – pride demon
Drystan - gluttony demon
Kieran - lust demon
Belial - envy demon

Astaroth - duke of Hell
Lily - witch, friend of alpha team
Franco - pride demon, Astaroth's assistant
Taylor - fae, friend of Rhys, damaged soul
Allocer - Duke of Hell, in charge of shadowlings
Mammon - Duke of Hell, in charge of new souls & demon children

Zadkiel - Angel of Righteousness
Raphael - Angel of Healing
Michael - Angel of Death

Constantine D'arius - vampire coven leader
Alpha Gregory - Alpha of the Albany pack
Felicity Bianchi - witch, Italy's coven leader

ACKNOWLEDGEMENTS

Oh, jeez. I have a bunch of people this wouldn't be the same without, but I want to give special thanks to Sarah for believing in me more than I believed in myself. Now, enough sappy, read on!

SYNOPSIS

Rhys

Getting my shit together shouldn't have been this hard. I'm making some progress—at a glacial pace—but I finally have my own place and I've left a twat waffle of a human being. I was even able to splurge on some real coffee and a Netflix subscription. Go me! I'm swearing off men forever. No more men problems for this boy!

So why do I feel so drawn to the deliciously tall drink of water knocking on my door, and why has no one locked him up for being fucking nuts? He turns my life upside down by showing me a world I could never have imagined. Now I have to learn to survive it, and if I'm lucky, I might be able to claim my man in the process.

Aridam

Tasked with tracking down some missing souls by my boss in Hell, I run into my fated mate . . . and he's *human*. No. This is not happening a second time.

I can't let him get caught up in the war brewing between vampires and the other supernaturals. I'll stick around just long enough to make sure he's safe, and introduce him to the supernatural world he might actually be a part of. Falling for him isn't in the cards . . . Too bad he doesn't much care for my carefully laid plans.

Chapter One

Rhys

Exhaustion looks good on exactly one person. Helena
Bonham Carter, in every movie she's ever been in. Other
than that? No one. I've got to be in the running for "the
biggest under-eye bags" award after this week, so I'm
feeling extra cranky. Moving into the new studio
apartment was quicker than I thought it would be. I
hadn't realized just how many of my things had been
quietly (and I guess sometimes pointedly) replaced over
the last year of living with my ex. It wasn't until I went to
load up the moving truck that it hit me. He'd thrown out
almost all of my furniture because his things were nicer,
better, newer. "You shouldn't waste money on clothes
since we are the same size and I can afford nicer threads."
His exact words, not mine. The nearly empty moving
truck was like a kick to the balls.

With a deep sigh, I look around and survey the new
(thrifted and gifted) furniture making up my space,
before heading to the bathroom. Eclectic is putting the
vibe my place gives off a little too nicely, and I feel my
stylish gay guy card wavering. I do really like a few pieces,
like the giant black mirror next to a burgundy bench in
the entry. A big fake-ass plant I don't know the origin of
completes the space, and amen to its lack of life because I

cannot take care of something unless it barks or cries when it's hungry.

I get to start completely fresh, and it's not like I have any family heirlooms to worry about. I roll my eyes at myself. *Damn, you sound like a bitter bitch.* When I was three, my mom died in a house fire that I survived only because she tossed me out our window before the roof collapsed. I know that much because of the news articles about it. It made some big headlines, apparently. I had poured over everything I could get my hands on once I was old enough to sneak into the public library after school.

Scrutinizing my face in the mirror, I see her brown eyes, unruly brownish-blondish hair, and thin nose looking back at me. My chin must have come from my dad, but I've never met him. No family came to claim me back then, so I stayed in foster care, bouncing around. No would-be family ever stuck. They were okay in the beginning, some better than others, but I seemed to matter less as time went on.

The second I aged out of the system, I was gone; I moved to New York to make something of myself (a godawful cliché but it's not wrong) and to follow my best friend to school. I haven't heard from any past foster parents since I left, and I haven't really expected to. At least at work I'm not invisible and I have a few friends. I haven't gotten very far financially, but I've been the happiest I've ever been. I mean, I thought I was. I drag my gaze away from the mirror and quickly brush my teeth and get ready for bed.

Working doubles at the club for the last few weeks to be able to afford the deposit on this dinky apartment was totally worth it. Thank God I got it as quickly as I did. A guy from work told me about the vacancy only hours after I caught *that asshole* balls deep in some twink in our bed. I shuffle over to the futon parading as a couch and collapse, grabbing the remote but unable to turn on the TV. My arm protests any kind of further movement. The bottles and kegs get heavy after countless hours lifting them, turning me into Jell-O after my shift.

My phone vibrates in my pocket. It has been going off almost constantly since I left while TA (that asshole) was at work. It's been days! What the ever-loving fuck does he think a simple phone call will change? The note I left should have taken care of it. I didn't hold a whole lot back. I will probably have to change my number, but that can wait until I have actual groceries in this place. Sasha (my bestie) will insist on the new number, but she's always hated him. It leaves a sour taste in my mouth that she was right. I hate it almost as much as I hate when she points it out. Her phrase "I told ya, Rhysies" never fails to rile me up. I'm definitely a snack, but we don't have to make my name sound like an admittedly delicious candy to prove it. Reece's Pieces, pfft. She even says it all stupid with the hard Es.

Even closing my eyes and pulling the blanket over my shoulders is a struggle. Just a little nap and I'll get up and be my normal snarky and fabulous self. Okay, maybe I'm more snarky and fabulous on the inside—the only thing outwardly showing I'm not just a regular guy's guy is painted toenails and my preference for colorful boy shorts versus plain briefs. I have three days off and refuse to waste them sleeping when I could park my fine ass on my couch (futon) and get back into my guilty pleasure series about some hot-as-hell vampires in Louisiana. The high-strung growly ones always get me going, and this series has a whole family of them.

I'm asleep before I can even set the remote back down on the ottoman.

Aridam

I gather as much patience as I can. Sitting in the lobby of my boss's office in Hell is not how I wanted to spend my day off. Astaroth never calls me to come in after hours, so I know it's important, but why am I waiting in this garish lobby? I fight not to roll my eyes at Stazie, a lower-level lust demon, as she sways her hips walking back to her desk. She's barking up the wrong tree, mostly. I'm pansexual—all demons are—but I have always leaned very heavily toward men. Less breakable.

Before I can wallow over the last person I slept with, Astaroth's personal assistant, Franco, walks briskly into the lobby and gestures for me to follow him. I stare at the back of his head until my gaze drops further, admiring the lines of his waist. Smaller than my usual type, he resembles a fae rather than a demon. I have to assume his Choice was practical instead of passionate. Low-level pride demons do make amazing employees if praised correctly. He leads me into a large office where my boss sits behind his sprawling black desk, looking polished but less pristine than I'm accustomed to seeing.

"Aridam, thank you for coming as swiftly as you did. I have something you need to look into immediately."

He hands me a list that has close to fifty names on it. I wait as patiently as I can for an explanation. I know this has something to do with mortals; otherwise, the whole team would be here. It's easier to send me in alone to do recon because Wrath only comes out on his own when in dire need or I choose it. The other demon types cannot control their sins; they leak them (pride, envy, etc.) all over the place. While each type of demon can be useful in day-to-day operations and large-scale missions, stealth is not exactly their forte. Maybe Kek, but he detests living in the shadows.

"I need you to go up top and check on these names. We have had an influx of shifter souls grace Reception recently. It intrigued me because there are no reports from the teams about shifter or supernatural unrest, so there is something going on. These names are what I need you to focus on. They appeared on the list at Reception, yet no soul showed up to represent them."

Growing visibly more agitated, he points to the top of the list in my hand. "You tell me why there are names showing up with no deaths attached to them. Where did the damned souls go? There are forty-seven names here. Four are fae and the rest are shifters. Figure out what is going on before Reception is overrun with angels demanding to know where their missing souls are. I cannot deal with Gabriel again this century without inciting a war. FIX. THIS!"

I try making sense of the names. The fae are the outliers and are probably why I'm getting this list and not some lower-level demons. Astaroth's mate is prophesized to be an elf, and he's waited for eight hundred years to meet them. The anomaly with Reception may lead to Astaroth actually finding his mate before his death . . . if his mate is actually wrapped up in this. The souls of the dead are always sent to Reception to await Judgement, and no living thing outside of angels or demons can enter Hell. He rarely leaves for obvious Duke of Hell reasons.

What happens after death sounds more complicated than it is. It was too dangerous (and honestly time consuming) to send all souls directly to The Gates of Heaven to be judged, just to kick most souls back over our way, anyway. Reception was built closer to Hell but is run by lower-level angels and neutrals. Souls are checked in and judged on a case-by-case basis. That way, soldiers and those who killed in self-defense aren't lumped in with serial killers or pedophiles. There is no pleading your case or arguing. Your entire life is projected at the speed of light for all in the Judgement Room to see and you are judged fairly by your own heart and mind, with neutrals mediating and making final decisions. Then the soul is taken to The Three Gates—a place where all three doors are located for convenience—and sent to the appropriate realm.

I assume Heaven and Neutral have a similar setup to Hell. (Purgatory is such an awful name for the truly neutral souls, and Neutral is better than "the grey area" like some dumbass suggested during the naming ceremony meeting.) First, there's an introductory period. Welcome to Hell, sentencing for crimes, the big Choice for your demon type, blah blah. It's overwhelmingly boring, but I had to learn. Being a high-level demon means I was born/created as a wrath demon, no Choice made here by yours truly. The plus side is that my soul is my own, not Hell's. My accomplishments are also my own doing, but there is no changing what I am or what rumbles inside me just barely contained. The designs on our wings make it easy to distinguish which level of demon you're talking to. . . as long as they're in demon form. Familiar hollow pain spreads through my chest and snaps me back to the present.

I nod briskly to Astaroth, rasping out a quick, "Yes, sir," before heading back out to the lobby. Pushing the side door open harder than necessary, I walk the familiar path to the garden. I need a moment before I go to the mortal realm. The noise is always too much at first. It takes a while for my human form to acclimate to my sensitive hearing. As a wrath demon, I am always poised for a fight, on an internal red alert. Makes sleeping a real pain. I can never turn it down enough to relax on Earth, so I'll need to account for resting here at the house every few names I track down. I don't need sleep in a traditional sense, but maybe once a week to just quiet my mind so I can focus and recharge more if I'm injured.

I see Astaroth at his office window, seeming to be looking over his faction, but I know he saw me the second I came out here. No more procrastinating. I head toward my room to change before I portal over. New determination hits me as I take a final look at our duke.

I'll do what I need to do. Astaroth may actually get some questions answered about the prophesy and what it means for his mate. It could all be connected to the names on this list. I can only wish him better luck with his mate than I had with mine.

Chapter Two

Rhys

"All right, I'm coming, damn!" Grumbling and stomping all the way to the door is what a person normally does on a Saturday night when their evening plans are interrupted, right? Never mind that I'm wearing tattered pajamas and haven't shaved in days. That's what they get for bursting my binge-watching, face-stuffing misery bubble. At least I'm less emotionally all over the place after some sleep and my phone has been going off less and less. I expect to find my best friend on the other side of the door in all her perky glory, begging me to come out and get over TA. Before the door is all the way open, I start forming my excuse to avoid clubbing, and stutter to a stop when I catch sight of who is actually standing in front of me.

This man is not Sasha (obviously), and honestly? I'm not complaining. I may be five foot ten, but I have to crane my neck to see his stupidly handsome face, my gaze about eye level with his nipples. Gah, I need a rag; I'm drooling all over myself. I must really need to get laid. My internal monologue has gotten positively pornographic if my half chub and intense perusal of his bulging muscles and exposed forearms are any indication. It's just so hard to find someone who wants to hold me down and . . . Wait, is he talking?

" . . . do you?"

Focus, Rhys! "Ummmmm . . . Do I what?" I *will* pull my gaze away from his nipples if it's the last thing I do. They're just RIGHT THERE. I swear one is pierced, but I cannot confirm without proper naked inspection, thank you very much, but you can't blame me for getting distracted.

"The guy who lives across the hall. Do you know where he is?"

Jealousy sparks through me with a vengeance. Taylor (pretty boy who lives in B3) is the definition of twink. All sugar and spice in a tiny package. Le sigh, if that is what this mountain of a man is looking for, I *really* don't make the cut.

Although I've recently (two seconds ago) decided Tay and I are mortal enemies, I'm still a little worried. "No, haven't seen him in a few days. Is everything okay?" The kernel of worry grows as the silence extends.

His eyes flash with something I don't quite catch, and he exhales roughly. "Yeah, that's all. Thank you for your time." He turns to leave in a rush and practically runs down the hall, tucking a small notepad into his back pocket. Damn, even his hands are big.

I stick my head out of the doorway so I can continue to watch his ass. "Are you a cop or something?" I call before he can completely disappear. He just keeps walking as if he didn't hear me. I stare at the empty hall for far too long before shutting the door again, and my chest twinges. Damn, I'd hate for that to be the last time I saw him. I didn't even get his name.

Aridam

My hands shake as I race down the stairs, my chest heaving with the effort of leaving him behind. I had just come to track down a name on the list; I hadn't asked for this. Why would I get another mate? He was perfect and smelled like sunshine, but he was HUMAN. I failed once with a witch, almost losing my life. Why would a fragile human ever choose me?! I'll stay away as long as I can. The pull will increase until we bond, making it physically hurt to be away from him. The longer we stay close, the harder it is to leave. I have to get away while I still can and at least report to Astaroth.

I whip out my phone and start dialing. My control on Wrath is slipping; the top of my head itches and my gums ache from my almost-transformation. Fuck, I need to hold on just until I can slip into an empty area before I portal home.

I see a door to the side of the front desk in the lobby and slip inside. Locked or not, it doesn't affect my ability to get in anywhere. All demons can do this unless a space is warded in some way. Lucky for me, there are no wards in sight, and I flick on the light to the empty maintenance closet as Astaroth□ picks up.

"Report," he barks.

"Nothing yet with the last fae name on the list, Taylor Winters. I have his scent from what I could gather from the apartment door. I'll track what I can and come back later to sweep the apartment after dark. His neighbor said he hasn't seen him for days." My chest tingles as I think about *him*. The hollow pain I had felt for decades faded into just an empty cavern some years ago.

Now even that has been replaced with the warmth of my new mate. I almost wish the feeling hadn't appeared; I was so used to loneliness. As much as I want to hide from him forever, I will have to find him again once I finish my current assignment. I know he will reject me once he figures out who I really am. I wonder how much time I'll have to take off work this go 'round so I can heal without harming anyone. Wrath pushes against my control even more, thrashing to get out and go claim his mate.
□ Astaroth interrupts my panicked spiraling.

"Find him. The new pattern means he has less than six months left before he enters Reception with no memory and his soul in tatters. He's the key, ☐ Aridam."

Before I can respond, the line goes dead. He's been increasingly short-tempered, and I have a feeling our faction of Hell is not having any fun with a pissed-off duke at its helm.

I need to contact the rest of the team and bring them in. With a quick thought, a portal shimmers against the wall in front of me, and I step through, walking into my private quarters on the team grounds. Stark emptiness and longing slam into me, begging me to go back. I lean against the wall to catch my breath and am assaulted with pieces of the night my first mate rejected me.

"You really are perfect, mate of mine." He had just started stripping down. We had been courting for weeks, and tonight, he wants to explore. Liam is a vision in his clothes, but my mouth positively waters with him out of them. We had taken this slow—well, slow by demon standards. I won't claim him tonight; he wants to wait until the moon is just right. I don't know when that will be, but I'm hoping soon. I want to make him mine.

"Take me, Aridam."

"Are you sure? I won't push you to do something before you're ready."

He chuckles. "Stop talking and mess me up already." He leans forward, nipping at my bottom lip. He tastes of tea and chocolate. I lose myself in my mate, being as gentle as possible with him.

He loses control at one point and slams down onto my cock, tearing a part of his tight hole. I try to stay his hips to give him time to adjust, but he whispers assurances against my lips and keeps riding me like he's dying without it.

After we both are milked dry, I fall asleep curled around him. When I wake, he's gone.

I shake off the memory. I don't need to rehash how it ended. Deep breaths. The more time that passes while I'm here, the easier it will become. In just a few minutes, I'm able to continue walking.

I shoot a quick message to the six other members of my team in our group chat as I finish changing. I immediately regret it because the feed gets either ignored or stuffed full of immature emojis as answers. If it weren't for Belial, we wouldn't be as advanced with human tech as we are. The emojis and slang are Azvameth's doing.

A few short minutes later, we all gather in our open floor plan common rooms. The only one missing is Az. As a sloth demon, he goes where he wants when he wants . . . at the pace he wants. For the most impatient guy on the team, he really takes his damned time. Belial offers to track him down, his voice carrying from the next room.

"He'll be here soon enough. It's not like we don't wait for everyone at some point." Devland, our resident greed demon, tosses out. He's not wrong per se; he just doesn't mention that we wait on Azvameth ninety percent of the time. It's always less than ten minutes, but it grates on all of our nerves.

While we wait, I take in the state of Drystan. I'm a little worried he won't be ready for whatever this assignment will bring. His skin is almost grey, like his demon is fighting to get out. Drystan never gives in and satisfies his need for gluttony. He will throw himself into one trend or another to 'help him find his center'. He hates a huge part of who he is, and that's a problem. Finding New Age ways to ignore it will only get us all killed. I believe the last time his gluttony was truly satisfied after going this long being starved was when he ate an entire village's supply of food, creating another third world country. If he would just let himself indulge more often, it wouldn't be this extreme. Next time it could start another world war if his gluttony fixates on death instead of just food, or an orgy country-wide somewhere if it's his sexual appetite that needs satisfaction.

I brush my hand in front of where Drystan's elbow rests on the small dining table, and he gives me a wink, his smile not quite reaching his eyes. Out of all of us, I'm closest to Drys. I'm the only one who can stop him when he fully unleashes his true form, but usually Wrath would rather be there right next to him, egging his gluttony on. He mouths *Later*, and I give the tiniest of nods. It can wait a little longer.

Az shuffles in and drops onto the couch closest to where I'm standing, draping himself over the arm like a king. "What are we waiting for?"

Kek can't help but get a jab in. "Start this mystery meeting, Oh Fearless Leader." His cutting voice masks the humor I see in his violet eyes. He may have wanted to be the head of this team, but after we told him his talents were wasted doing bureaucratic bullshit, he jumped to agree. Thankfully that reasoning worked with him, and he realized the team would be an utter shitshow if he ran it. I nod and roll my eyes. I would have thanked him if he had been a bit less sarcastic; praise goes quite a long way with Kek.

I fill them in as best I can, leaving out the parts about my new mate. Kieran and Kek head out immediately to do a full sweep of Taylor's apartment. They'll be quick, and Kek will keep Kieran out of trouble. The little one really can't help it. Lust trickles out of him constantly, making humans become enthralled in minutes, stalkers in hours, and crazed maniacs if in contact with him for a few days.

Drystan heads my way as the others disperse to jump on their own tasks. I jerk my chin toward the balcony close by, and we head that way. Stepping outside, I feel the warmth of our dark-red sun; the faint scent of smoke and home fills my lungs.

"What are you hiding, Ari? There's something you're not telling us."

I hate that he's right. "I found him, Drys."

His eyes widen. "Who? Taylor? Then why are we—?"

"No, no, not that. My . . . mate." I whisper so low at the end that Drystan has to lean in to catch it.

"No fucking way. You're not going back there. Are you crazy? He rejected you! Got your giant dumb ass banished!"

I resist the urge to slap a hand over his loud mouth. "Shut up! Not him. He died like twenty or thirty years ago, I think. That was when the pain changed. I felt the mating pull when I was up there tracking down the Winters fae."

"What happened? Why are you here and he isn't? You did something really stupid, didn't you?"

I shrug and look away. "It's not that easy. You cannot imagine how hard it was to walk away, but it needed to

23

happen. He is *human*, Drys. How am I meant to take a chance on something so fragile? Just telling him about demons would kill him. There's no way I can survive a mate rejection again and still function for this assignment."

"I think you're being really fucking stubborn. I'll give you until this assignment is over before I go up there and see for myself what you're passing up."

"Don't go near him!"

"Well now, why do you care? If you don't want him, someone else will," he snarks out before spinning and walking back inside like he hasn't just thrown a match onto an already unstable fire.

I stalk after him, but Belial stops me. He obviously has something to tell me that he can't put into a text or email. I brace myself for the onslaught of envy. It's impossible to resist after about ten minutes, but I try my damnedest because none of this is his fault.

"When you go back, I think you should take a look at the wolf shifter pack closest to Winters's apartment. They've been having shifters go missing but haven't reported it themselves. A human not in the know always ends up calling the cops and filing a report. I've gotten into the pack's financials, and there are some huge discrepancies, Aridam. Being paid one hundred thousand dollars for hay? It's New York. They don't even have livestock registered. I would be surprised if they were able to keep animals; they normally freak the beasties out."

That really could have gone into an email; it must be nice to go around doing whatever you want. It's not like we have bigger things to worry about. He never worries, though, does he? He shouldn't be in charge of the tech; it's too important a job. What was I thinking, putting him in charge of that? To be that oblivious and still get all the glory when an assignment runs smoothly. Like we did nothing. I'd give—shit! Okay, that's not me. I shake my head to clear the buzzing anger and envy roiling around in there. A deep breath doesn't really help, but I'm able to force words out.

"Understood. Good work, Bel." He dips his head and rushes off. I sigh in relief, then feel terrible. He has to live this way. Fucking angels.

Now that I have a new lead, I'll be able to throw myself into work and avoid thinking about my mate.

- - -

The air smells like stale fear and wet dog. I know it's considered derogatory to compare wolf shifters to dogs, but it's genuinely what they smell like to demons. I haven't spent a lot of time with human pets, but Devland assures me the description is accurate.

It's a little quieter than I would assume pack lands would be. Normally they're a boisterous bunch. I wait for the she-wolf I managed to get a message to to show up. She's mated to one of the alpha's enforcers. Apparently since his mate died, the alpha has been going off the rails. It's normal for someone to go feral after losing a mate, but he isn't showing the normal signs. More cold and ruthless than grieving widower.

I sense her presence before she speaks softly. "I can't stay long. I have only a minute. A heck of a lot of visitors have been here recently, and it's put the pack on edge."

I can read between the lines pretty well. "Oh? Have you had the pleasure of meeting any of them?"

"No, they come in toward dusk and meet with our alpha alone. I've only heard one name, and it's because he's the . . . leader."

"Look, I'm impressed by your ability to talk around the issues, but I really just need you to speak plainly."

"I'm sorry, demon, I cannot do as you request."

Compulsion. Fuck. I try again.

"Does this have anything to do with the missing shifters?"

"I cannot say." Her eyes well with tears.

"Can you give me the name of the vampire who compelled you?"

"I cannot say."

"Have you ever met them before they were in talks with your alpha?"

"No."

"Is their coven near here?"

"I cannot say." Which means yes?

"Do you know what's happening to the shifters?"

"I cannot s—Wait. I can say I don't have a real working knowledge. Just a theory."

I nod at her to continue.

"They have never sent a shifter back after requesting 'help' with building something. They're very specific in their employment requirements each time, but not in general. Strong, weak, old, young."

"How often do you receive 'employee requests' normally?"

"Every month."

"When will the next request be, do you think?"

"We had our strongest shifter transfer to their employment six days ago."

Shit. Okay. So we have some time but not a lot if we want to find them alive, and too much time to wait it out until the next request.

"I must go back now, but please, please help us. There aren't many who haven't been taken under . . . influence here, though most don't remember."

"Do you think your alpha is under this influence?"
 "No." It's all she says before running back the way she came.

I portal back home and go searching for Belial.

Chapter Three

Rhys

I sip the sweet caffeinated nectar of the gods at the Starbucks right down the street from my apartment, watching people flit in and out of the shop while I wait for Sasha to meet me for our weekly date. I'm a little early, but I have been feeling off for weeks now, even worse than after TA cheated on me. Thinking of TA happens less and less. His phone calls stopped a few days ago. I still can't believe I had actually met the guy he cheated with; he worked with my ex at this big accounting firm. Those "late hours" seem like such bullshit now.

Anyway, I've been off. It's an overwhelming feeling, like I'm not where I'm supposed to be, really restless, and my chest hurts at odd times. I even went to a free clinic before work last week because I thought I was having a heart attack at first. They found nothing; I have a clean bill of health.

I'm not left with any more time to ponder my aches and pains as Sasha sweeps into the shop with her signature look: bright billowy skirt, white cropped shirt, stunning blue eyes, and red hair in crazy natural curls reaching just past her shoulders. She waves before quickly getting in line and then heading straight for me after placing her order.

"I missed you on Saturday! One of these weeks, we'll finally get you to come out again. It's been forever, Rhysies."

"Hmm," I murmur noncommittally, raising an eyebrow and waiting her out. I know there's more here because she is acting twitchier and perkier than normal.

"Don't give me that face. I hate that face!" Her nose scrunches. "Ugh, fine, we'll pretend you've appropriately adjusted and are getting back out there." Her name is called from the pickup window. "Oh! Hold that thought." She rushes to grab her latte and is back before I can even think to make an escape.

"Anyway! I have news! Colin and I are moving in together! Isn't that great?! We decided to give up our apartments and look at houses a little farther from the city. Now, I know it'll be an adjustment, but we'll still talk just as much, and weekly coffee dates are a go . . ." She rambles on a little more, barely breathing since she's talking so fast. Likely trying to convince both of us that nothing will change. It will, silly girl, but I couldn't be happier for her.

"That's great, Sash! Have you looked at many places?" I give her the easy out, and her shoulders drop in clear relief. We talk more about little things like décor and make plans for later this week to go through her apartment to get rid of anything she won't need for their new place. As we stand from the table, I give her a kiss on the cheek and hug her a little tighter than normal as we leave the shop. I grin as she waves dramatically and gets into her cherry-red mini cooper, and swallow a lump in my throat, heading back to the apartment.

- - -

As I open the lobby door, the pain in my chest starts again, and I try rubbing it away. It hasn't helped before, but I can't help but do it again. My mind is so focused on the pain that I get to the stairs and just can't muster the want to trudge up them today, my plan to keep my ass in tip-top shape be damned. I turn to head toward the elevator and stop dead. Swinging my head around like a crazy person, I start freaking out.

Why is no one moving? I was so lost in my head that I didn't see the lady who lives a floor below me and her tiny Pomeranian both frozen two steps up on the left . . . or the older couple holding hands mid-step by the mailboxes. I can't see or hear anyone move at all. Fear trickles down my spine. The silence is unnatural as all hell, and I feel the urge to flee but have no idea where I'd go. Up to my apartment or back outside?

Before I can decide, I see a flicker of something out of the corner of my eye and snap my head to the right. The same guy who had asked about Taylor steps into the lobby from one of the mystery doors that are always locked. There goes my hope that this might just be the start of a super creepy flash mob or something.

He looks just as edible as last time, with a nicely tailored suit instead of the casual biker bad-boy vibe he was throwing off before. We lock eyes and continue to stare at each other. I take a step forward almost involuntarily, and he turns to look out onto the street, the giant wall of old-school windows giving off enough of a reflection for me to see that he's scowling. I crack first, scared he'll leave.

"What is going on?" It's all I can think of saying, because surely *Hey, are you a serial killer? Cause if not, I'd like to see your dick and maybe sit on it* isn't something that should pop out of my mouth. Fuck, I'm losing my mind. All I can think of is him, though the whole frozen-people thing is a pretty close second.

He swings his head around at the sound of my voice, silver-grey eyes narrowing as he runs his hand through his inky-black hair for what looks to be the hundredth time.

"You shouldn't be here. It's not safe." I just blink at him until he sighs and continues. "Fine, let's go." I sidle up next to him, touching his suit jacket before he can take it back. My chest feels all warm and has been tingling since he started talking. What is happening here? I just want to sink into him and feel safe, though all signs point to this entire situation being anything but.

"Where are we going?" He just starts walking at a clipped pace back out the front door of the building. I hurry to follow, walking next to him but unable to keep my mouth shut. "What was that back there? Science gone wrong? Oh! Maybe a chemical bomb? Like liquid nitrogen but gas form? It was, wasn't it? Damn. Aren't you going to wait for backup? You're a cop, right?" I glance up at his perfectly shaped lips, his cupid's bow pronounced and his plump bottom lip just begging to be nibbled.

"No? Alrighty then. Not a cop. A PI?" Nothing. "Not much of a talker, are you?" I give him plenty of time to answer any of the questions I just word vomited all over him. We reach the street, and it seems completely normal, like nothing happened twenty feet behind us. I try to be patient and wait another beat, and he's still quiet, facing straight ahead and giving no indication he even heard me. Do I need to be louder? "I'M RHYS! WHAT'S YOUR NAME?"

He lurches his head away from my yelling and looks at me incredulously like it's my fault he may have a busted ear drum. It's not, by the way; it's rude to ignore questions when creepy shit is happening . . . and his hearing is fine, I think.

"Ari," he growls out. The frustration on his face only enhances his frown lines and his stellar fucking cheekbones that I'd die to have. He looks like an angry mob boss from a movie.

"Are you in the mob?" I blurt out, and feel my face and neck heat. Man, this filter thing is breaking quick today. I should work on that.

"What? No. Why did you—you know what? Never mind." He looks forward again as we cross the street. He walks like people will just jump out of the way, and they do! As an average guy walking across the street, I get bumped into constantly by people staring at their phones, but for him, people part like the Red Sea.

"No, seriously, where are we going?"

"To see a friend." He doesn't even look my way. Kind of disappointing.

"Friend? You gotta give me more than that, big guy."

He huffs in annoyance and stops abruptly. "If you want to go back, feel free. If you want to be safe, stick by me and listen when I tell you to do something, no matter how crazy it sounds. And no more questions, got it? We don't have time."

I stare at him; this is the longest he's talked the entire time. Usually it's grunts and silence. "Fine. Yeah, okay . . . I'll try." That's the best I can do. He nods and starts walking again. I almost have to jog to keep up.

After what feels like forever (probably thirty minutes but I've hit my workout quota for the week already so I'm breathing embarrassingly heavy while trying to pretend I'm fine), he slows and grabs my wrist to stop me. A tingle shoots straight up my arm, and my breath catches. His eyes fly to mine and hold. This pull I feel toward him makes me crazy. I feel hot all over, and the tingle has migrated from my arm straight to my dick. I whimper and shiver from the feeling. He seems to snap out of it, dragging me into a shop with no sign out front, the bell dinging as we walk in. I've never been in a witchy shop before, but this is exactly what I would picture one looking like. The smell is strong but comforting, like incense and . . . dirt? If that makes any sense. Sasha would say "earthy," but it doesn't smell like nature, just dirt.

Ari waits by the counter, and I decide to look around to give myself some space to try to calm my erection down a little. It's not really working. He's a needy fucker, apparently, when it comes to Ari. The man even breathes in my direction and I get a stiffy, and I really don't need a wet spot forming for seemingly no reason. A big black stone with a slight grey swirl sits on a stand of sorts, and I want to get a closer look at the swirl . . . maybe there's more on the back.

"Don't touch anything!" he snaps at me as I reach to pick it up.

"I'm not!" I was. "I didn't even touch it!" I was going to.

His glare intensifies, and I shudder again. Growly is such a turn on. I have a pretty healthy libido normally, but this is getting out of hand. His eyes darken and, if I'm not mistaken, turn heated. A woman glides in all graceful and shit, like she didn't just interrupt a good eye-fucking. I should shank her with the black rock I picked up anyway. I don't listen all that well outside the bedroom. Inside it, I'm a good boy.

The welcoming smile on her face drops when she spots Ari over by the desk. Her brows snap down. "What do you want? Get out! I told you never to come back here." My face must betray my shock, because she turns to me. "And is this your fault? Why would you bring him back here? I banished his ass a long time ago."

What the hell is she talking about?

"Wha—?"

"He didn't bring me; he's in danger." He still looks calm, almost disinterested.

They seem to now be having a pretty intense staring contest, neither looking away or blinking. I have to interrupt or I will die of old age before I get any answers.

"I am so lost here. I thought we were going to see your friend? I know you said no more questions, but . . ." I aim the question paired with an innocent look at Ari.

"Yes, demon, care to explain?"

Did she say demon? Rude. Sure, he doesn't seem like the most likable guy, but name-calling is a little far. A rush of something crashes over me, like I need to protect him even if it's from an insult.

"What's your name?" I demand. Better to get her focus on me.

Aridam

"My name is Lily Stronghold and this is my shop. You're new to this world, right?" Not waiting for an answer, she directs her next question to me. "What does he know so far?"

I squirm, feeling like this might blow up in my face, and mutter the confession almost under my breath.

"Nothing?! Nothing at all? You drag an unknown and uninformed human into my shop?"

Well, shit, she's not wrong. I glance at Rhys. He's almost shaking and still clutching the obsidian sphere like a shield. Out of everything in the shop, why pick the one that has healing, protection, and truth-telling properties? I narrow my eyes. Is he a witch too? He doesn't have the electric scent of one, so maybe he knows the more traditional spiritual crystals and grabbed it on a hunch?

Lily nudges me and waves her hand like she expects more information from me, but I can't do anything but stare at my mate and blink. His face is so expressive, and I wish I could see him in more tender moments, but I know this is as far as I can take him. I've already been close to him for too long. Leaving will hurt immensely, but it's what's best for him. I can't be the mate he needs; I won't do this again.

I stand frozen in the middle of a shop Liam asked me to meet him at. I'm being held by a livid witch spewing nonsense. I could smack myself for not checking for a salt circle. How stupid.

"You dare enter my shop after you assault one of mine?! You vile creature. Liam has asked for sanctuary and I will grant it. I will do a hell of a lot more than that." The witch's tone is scathing.

38

"Assault? He's my mate! I would never—"
"I saw the evidence of your brutality myself! You dare deny he left your care bleeding? That he begged for you to wait? What kind of mate does that?"

"No! I mean, yes, but—" I scramble to make sense of what is happening.

"Liam! Let's get this part done." Her face is a mask of righteous fury.

My mate enters the room, eyes red rimmed like he's been crying. What is going on? "Liam? What happened?"

"What do you mean, what happened? You brutalized me. Terrorized me for weeks, forcing me to bend to your will. I cannot be your mate. I won't!" Shock spreads through me. I never laid a hand on him. I was respectful of every single boundary. I look back at every moment and find nothing. Last night, he was the aggressor. He was the one who threw himself onto my cock, fighting the comfort I tried to give him when he hurt himself.

I stand there, dumbfounded. "What are you talking about? You—"

"I, Liam Engelmann, reject you, Aridam, as my mate."

Pain sears through me, buzzing in my ears and preventing me from hearing the witch Lily speak at first.

"—banished once, banished twice, and thee be banished to Hell for a full century. So mote it be."

The world spins around me and I fall.

I strengthen my resolve. "I was hoping Lily would be able to teach you about our world. I cannot stay, but we can't have you walking around still uninformed. She's an experienced teacher and witch, one of the most powerful I've met.

I turn to her. "He needs to know everything, and I'm pretty sure he's a Null based on today. He would have found out eventually, anyway. This way, we know he is in the right hands and protected . . . and lastly, you owe me." That's quite the understatement considering I couldn't step foot on Earth for well over a century because she took Liam's word over mine.

She tilts her head at me. "And that's all? That's the only reason?" Damn her. I'm even more certain she can sense bonds as part of her gifts now.

I give a subtle nod at her unspoken question. "I would like you to keep that information to yourself while teaching him . . . please." Manners never hurt in this kind of situation.

She heaves a sigh and turns back to Rhys. "Come, child, let's get you fed."

That seems to be Rhys's breaking point. He takes a huge breath and lets loose. "I feel like I've been pretty damn calm about everything that's happened so far today even though I'm freaking the fuck out. You said no more questions, but I cannot handle this. Meatloaf! Red! Whatever safe word I need to say to get off this fucking ride, because I don't like or understand what's happening. First, why were those people frozen? Why is no one else losing their shit? There's no way you guys are friends, 'cause you don't act like it, and now you're talking like I'm not even in the room, mentioning demons, 'your world,' witches, and banishing! The fuck is a Null?

"And YOU! What do you mean you can't stay? You're going NOWHERE without my bitchy ass unless you want me to shank you where you stand, you overgrown, lying, Adonis's-evil-twin-brother fuckstick! I followed you here because I felt like I should trust you, and I nearly always listen to my gut, SO tell me what the FUCK. IS. GOING. ON!" His voice rises to a near-screeching level and his face turns almost purple as he goes on.

Lily rushes to reassure him, but I haven't been able to gather enough words to form a sentence. I feel my jaw hanging open and quickly snap it shut. I breathe in deep and make a decision I'm sure I'll regret in the morning, but I can't leave him while he's so upset.

"I can stay and explain as much as I can tonight. I'm on assignment right now, so you cannot accompany me. It's dangerous, Rhys, and I won't be able to do what I have to if I'm worried about your safety."

"Swear that you will explain everything? That you'll come back?" His chin wobbles and my chest caves in. I must hesitate for just a moment too long, because the hope starts to fade from his enchanting chocolate eyes.

Quickly, I blurt, "I swear to you!" and his answering smile lights up everything around him. With a start, I realize I'd do anything to see him like that always. Shaking off the fanciful thoughts, I look to Lily.

"Why don't we get settled and I show you where you'll be staying, Rhys? Then we can see about scraping together a quick meal. You must be starving." She goes to steer him by his elbow, turning them both away from me.

He grumbles about not forgetting she called him a child but is obviously swayed by her second offer of food. They head down the hallway toward the stairs up to her apartments above the shop; I pull out my phone to give Astaroth a quick update via text. Best not to call him else he finds something in the tone of my voice that reveals I'm hiding something.

Chapter Four

Rhys

"So you're telling me a soul walks into a reception area and checks in? Like a hotel? Mhmm, okay." It's too bad one of the sexiest men I've ever seen is a lunatic. I think my brain is broken, because instead of being even more freaked out, I just love listening to him talk.

He gazes at me in frustration. It's a look I've grown accustomed to in the past few hours of explanation. "That's what you're hung up on? Not that I'm a demon with another form, but the soul process?"

"Oh, we'll get to that, make no mistake." I have so many questions, but now all I can think about is how he might get naked to 'show me'. "Actually, now is better. I wanna see!" I've already called off of work for a family emergency for the next few days at Lily and Aridam's urging so I can sift through this new info.

"No."

My hand twitches in my lap. "What? Why? Is it the whole 'if I show you I'll have to kill you' thing?" If he isn't mob, he must be CIA.

"I would never hurt you." He looks so offended, I can't help but snicker.

"Well, then lemme see! Otherwise, it'll hurt my feelings and you just said you wouldn't hurt me." I pout, pulling out the best puppy eyes I can muster. I add in a kernel of truth just in case he sees through my bullshit. "It'll also help prove that you aren't as cocoa puffs as logic is telling me you are, hot or not." Now, when nothing happens, I can say I tried. Do they have conjugal visits in the place with grippy socks?

He reluctantly stands to his full height. His eyes screw shut and nothing happens, naturally. I look away and reach to pat him on the arm. "It's okay, Ari, I—" Movement under my hand makes me pause and glance at him, doing a double take. "Holy shit!"

His grey eyes seem to shine like liquid silver. Two blackened horns the size of my forearm curve out of the top of his forehead. Fangs poke out from under his top lip, mouth open slightly. He's grown just a bit, close to eight feet now. His skin has a reddish hue and feels a little rough.

I stand and take a step forward. "Holy shit," I whisper. Apparently those are the only words I know now. I reach up to touch his face, and he eyes me warily. Over his shoulder are massive black leathery wings that flex like they're restless, covered in an intricate design. I'm a little sad the pants he had changed into proved to be so stretchy. My eyes snag on the bulge cradled between two thighs the size of tree trunks. My mouth waters as the fabric strains even more, the bulge growing under my gaze. My knees feel weak, like I should be kneeling on them instead of trying to stay standing like an idiot.

Am I a freak for being this turned on? Frankly I don't give a damn after five more seconds of mapping him with my eyes. I tilt my head back, trying to look at the rest, practically begging for permission to put my mouth on him. He cups my jaw so gently, at odds with the violence his body looks to be made for. I can feel the strength practically vibrating under his skin. My left hand travels south, gliding over the confirmed nipple piercing while my right traces the indents around his muscles leading to his belly button.

"Rhys," he croaks, like talking takes all his strength. He backs up, causing my hands to drop along with my heart. Ari spins around, and his skin returns to normal (I mean, normal for me?) and his wings seem to snap back into his shoulder blades. "I need a minute." He takes off onto the balcony right off the living room of Lily's apartment. I feel unsteady, sinking into the cushions of the black leather couch.

Lily floats into the room and hands me a mug. I can only assume it's tea or coffee (hopefully the latter). I sip the hot liquid, letting it ground me as my brain finally catches up to what my body has been telling me. It's real. *It's all real.* I feel dizzy, the coffee not working as well as I'd hoped. I need Ari. I just want him to hold me and tell me everything will be okay. I don't know when he became my life raft in the single day I've known him, but I've come to depend on his grunts and scowls. His steady, unwavering presence . . . though I definitely understand he's totes the one who rocked the boat in the first place. I look over to the balcony as he comes back in, seeming stiff and speaking more formally—a nervous habit, I assume.

"I must get going. I will return as swiftly as I can. Please let Lily instruct and protect you while I'm gone. You cannot contact me while I'm away. However, I should be back within a week . . . perhaps two. Do not go to work; do not tell anyone where you are."

I had already told Sasha I was going out of town, so other than her and work, I don't know who he would think I'd contact. A therapist? I should probably see one of those here soon.

"Now? You're leaving now? I thought you would leave in the morning?" I feel close to begging him to stay.

"I got a lead and have to check it out quickly."

I can almost feel the lie. It's probably mostly true, but something about it rings false. I don't really have time for a response as he walks to the room he was going to crash in tonight. I get up to follow after I feel steadier, but Lily stays me with a hand on my shoulder.

"He's already gone." Huh? Oh, right, portals. That's a thing now. I sigh as tears well in my eyes. My chest hurts so damned bad. It hasn't been giving me trouble since this morning, but my luck has run out, I guess. I'll probably have a heart attack or stroke before he gets back.

Lily pulls me up gently and leads me into the kitchen, handing me a new mug. This time, it's a bitter tea. I can't hide my grimace.

"It's a healing tea. It will help with the pulling in your chest while he's gone."

"What?"

"The chest pain, child. It's from your bond growing stronger, yes? It will physically hurt to be away from him for a while. Should get better with some time. Maybe a few hours now."

"It can't be. It's been happening for weeks."

"Before or after you met him?"

I think back. "Umm . . . after, definitely after."

"Let me explain a little more. You seem confused, and that demon has a giant issue with communication. I will not keep you in the dark about yourself; it would only make things worse."

"Yeah . . . if you could make sense any time soon, that'd be great," I snark.

She gives me a warning glare, almost like the one I imagine a mother would give. "First I need to explain what you are so you can understand the why of everything else, yes?" She waits for a nod from me before continuing. "A Null is someone impervious to any magic not naturally occurring in nature. Example—a spell to make vines spring a trap onto a trespasser will not activate if you were to walk over it, but if you are holding a healing crystal, its natural magic will work. This also means you cannot be compelled; magical attacks like the one in your building will skip you like it did today. Following? Good. If you think about all the implications, you can see how dangerous someone like you is."

I open my mouth to protest, but she puts up her hand. "I don't mean you hurting anyone directly. Rhys, you can walk into a room full of supernaturals and not a single thing they do will hurt you unless they use their own hands or mortal weapons, no magic. You are the ultimate weapon for thieves and monsters, but a brilliant scout for the good guys. That's why you need to start taking care of yourself. We start basic hand-to-hand tomorrow."

Lily releases a huge sigh and allows a pregnant pause before she asks, "What do you know about mates?"

Aridam

Once I no longer feel like passing out, I head toward the common room again to update the team and see where Dev and Bel are at with their online info gathering. Anything to go on will be helpful. I've been trying to focus on finding info on Taylor Winters, but everything comes back to Rhys. His soft smile and the way my skin tingles everywhere he touches. I had to leave or I would have bent him over the nearest surface. The urge to claim my mate had pounded in my ears, the scent of his arousal making it hard to breathe. I wanted to hear him scream my name, to hold him down and fuck him until his insides molded to my cock.

"Aridam!"

I snap back to the now, and the frustrated look Devland gives me is like a bucket of ice water. Fuck, I need to get it together. From the sound of it, that wasn't the first time he had called my name.

"My mind was elsewhere. What did you guys find?" I brush off Belial's concerned look and hold Devland's searching gaze.

With a sigh, he shakes his head. "Nothing. And it's not like we couldn't find anything useful. More like he never existed. No birth records, social media, employment history, nada. Not even tax records, and you know how stringent human governments are about keeping track of what they feel like their people owe them. The address we got on him before is gone too."

"We will need to do more old-school work on this one." Belial looks pained just saying it.

"Yes! It's my turn!" Kieran skips into the room with a wide smile. "I can talk to more of the humans we know had contact with him. Maybe start with the neighbor you already talked to. You know humans can't resist giving me info." He winks.

My mind snaps at the thought of Kieran anywhere near Rhys. Wrath slips out and grabs him by the neck, slamming him against the wall by the door he had just come through. "MINE!" he roars.

"Whoa, man. Didn't mean anything by it." His attempt at pacifying Wrath does very little, but it does allow me enough leeway to wrestle control back from the red haze filling my vision. I don't know what to tell him when I let go, the stares of my team burning holes into my back. He coughs and adjusts his clothing, smoothing the wrinkles from his shirt.

"I—" I can't think of anything to explain my behavior except the truth, so I say nothing, flexing my hands by my side. "I apologize."

"That's it? Damn, Aridam, it's not like you to lose control. You need to tell us what has your panties in a twist," Kek chimes in. I am really off my game. I didn't notice him arrive.

"Let's just focus on Winters and let me worry about Wrath, all right?" My statement is met with some palpable skepticism, not that I blame them.

"Drystan and I will follow up on the covens in the area, going off the lead I got from the Albany pack. Closest to the pack first, if possible. Kek and Kieran, since you teamed up and tossed his place, follow the strongest scent and track down where he went last if you can. Devland and Belial, keep hunting for info; it can't *all* be completely gone. If Azvameth deigns to make an appearance, tell him I'd appreciate if he'd check out the club Winters worked at." Drystan looks a little better than he did the last time I saw him. His skin isn't as sallow or grey. He must have gorged on something semi-recently.

We need to get this done in the next few days or I will completely lose my hold on Wrath. Who knows what he'll do to Rhys if I can't temper him. Visions of him split on my true form's cock fill my head, his soulful brown eyes glassy as he writhes beneath me. I can almost hear him

51

begging. I need to mark him from the inside so everyone knows he's mine.

I can feel my dick, hard and leaking . . . in a room full of demons that can scent my arousal. There's no way the others missed it. They apparently decide to ignore it, splitting off to tackle their orders. Drystan hovers a few strides away, looking anywhere but at me. "Fuck, let's go." He smirks at my tone but says nothing.

- - -

Constantine D'arius is an elder vampire I've had the displeasure of meeting exactly once. Arrogant purist, looking down on everyone. Fool of a man who believes he's the oldest, and therefore strongest, in the room.

Vampires aren't to be taken lightly, even as fledglings. They're incredibly intelligent since knowledge is passed down from their sires as they go through their transformation. A very traditional race when it comes to ranking and age (age past transition, not mortal life), though pretty modern in terms of gender equality. No one is as old as they look since they stop aging when they're turned. Their ability to manipulate their energy makes other supernaturals extremely uneasy because they can dampen it, making themselves seem like less of a threat. The reverse doesn't work . . . they cannot increase their power signature to appear more dangerous. Makes sense to help them hunt and stalk their blood sources, but no predator likes to go in blind thinking someone is prey because they seem weaker, only to get their throat ripped out. At times, you can sense they are vampires, but little past that unless they allow you to feel it.

From what I know, vampires do not have mates in the traditional sense. They can choose one donor to gift a naturally immortal lifespan to as long as they blood share with them. It will not change the mortal, just keeps their blood source going. It creates a bond based more on survival since the blood bonded can still be killed, and vamps are protective of their food. When I met Constantine before, he was lecturing a group of baby vamps about bonding and how doing so makes you weak. That not hunting creates laziness and it's not allowed in his coven. I hated him on sight, how he looked at Kieran with unusual interest. Like a meal, not just with lust. I shiver as I recall his beady eyes latching on to Kieran's neck, almost salivating. I almost hope he has the souls so I can end him.

"Anything?" I ask Drystan as we creep to the outer edges of Constantine's estate grounds, keeping my voice to near subvocal levels. Being quiet doesn't do much good since they can hear hearts beating for miles, but keeping the element of surprise as long as possible is always nice. We thought we caught a whiff of the fae's scent in the woods a block or so away.

"Nothing. I can't pick up any mortal scents, either."

My mind stutters at what he's saying. "No human blood?" We aren't that far away. There should be *something* with how many vamps reside here with Constantine. These woods are surely used as hunting grounds for the newly transitioned until they can control the bloodlust.

He gives me a blank stare. I refuse to look sheepish for second-guessing him, so I open myself up. I get nothing. "Okay, I can't sense anything, either; I double checked. I thought maybe I was distracted and wasn't picking up what I should have been."

A snap a ways off catches our attention. A group of vampires are about a mile away, masking energy. I do a quick inventory. With both Drystan and I, we can fairly easily take on the thirty vampires I sense as long as there are no extra surprises. We communicate in a form of ASL, something I'm glad Kek insisted we all learn. I signal for him to take the right half while I take the left. After a brief nod, we run out of time.

The tree line bursts with sudden activity as vampires rush out, clearing the distance in mere seconds. I had enough time to let Wrath out, a red haze settling over my eyes. Fury pulses through my veins as my claws extend, wings snapping out to the side in tandem with my barbed tail. Movements blur; I can only feel the sprays of blood from my attackers as it washes over me. Occasional grunts pass my lips as a few of their hits land, one in particular sinking into my shoulder blade.

It takes less than ten minutes before Drystan and I are the only ones left standing, the wreckage of downed limbs and blood-sprayed earth giving one heck of a backdrop to our heaving chests. The haze lifts, and I swing my now smaller body toward my teammate. Drys looks a little battered but gives a satisfied smile.

"I got seventeen; looks like you're losing your edge."

I scoff. I can't believe he counted, though if he had fully released gluttony, I doubt I would have even gotten the thirteen I did. "Oh, fuck off," is what I meant to say, but instead, I slur a little and stagger to the side, feeling incredibly tired. Drystan's face is out of focus, but I can see his lips moving, his words sounding warbled. I open my mouth to assure him I'll be fine and it doesn't even hurt, when everything goes black.

Chapter Five

Rhys

It's been a week since Ari left and I can still feel the pain in my chest. It's not as bad, but a constant dull ache that a-fucking-pparently comes with a MATE BOND. I swear when I see Ari next, I'm going to smack his perfect fucking face. How could he not tell me? I get it. Liam was a grade-A douche canoe from what Lily told me, but I'm not like him. *How would he know that?* Maybe because I want to ride his demon dick, not banish him. Instead of telling me I'm not crazy pants for thinking about how it would feel to lick his horns, he *leaves me!*

I shake my inner ranting, forcing myself to focus on what Lily is trying to explain.

"—and then you can push it down." She looks up, expecting a reaction, I'm assuming.

"Uh . . . great!" Her eyes narrow. I sigh. Fucksicles, wrong answer.

"Focus, child! If someone is coming at you, you need to know how to use this or you'll end up hurting yourself instead."

I take in the small staff she is holding. "Okay, I'm sorry. I'll pay better attention, I swear!"

After she is satisfied that I can remember the whole two steps to opening the staff, she turns me to face a boxing dummy set up against the wall of the building outside. "Now you hit. It has a long reach, so you have more control when you focus your movements with your wrist and not the whole arm." She adjusts my hold and has me flick it out, starting small.

Twenty minutes later, I'm soaked in sweat but have a better handle on how to use different parts of my body to control it and how much force to use. I trudge inside. Stepping into the kitchen, I have an immense sense of dread. I look around quickly, surveying the space. Nothing. A shimmery blur thing starts by the stove, and I have my staff out and ready. It looks like a portal, maybe. Lily tried to describe them, but I don't know if that's what I am looking at here. More importantly, I have no idea what is going to come through if I'm right unless they are so impressed by my ability to open a staff that they surrender.

A giant demon with smooth grey skin and dark patterned wings steps out, and I squeak in a very *manly* way, fear sneaking down my spine as I straighten to swing at him. I then notice what he is carrying. It's Ari.

"No! No, no, no . . ." I keep repeating as I rush over to him. "What happened?" I push Ari's silky black hair out of his eyes. *So much for smacking.*

"Obsidian blade. I need someone to remove it quickly!" I slip my hand around to where he had gestured with his chin, and run into something warm and sticky. "Oh God." It's Ari's blood. I feel around, but everything is so slippery, I can't get a good grip on the thing protruding from his back. I look around frantically for somewhere to lay him so I can get to the wound.

"Put him here!"

Mystery man tosses Ari face and stomach first onto the kitchen island like a rag doll. I wince at the impact, but since Ari hasn't even flinched, I assume he's out cold.

"I can't remove it myself; you have to hurry before he bleeds out."

That kicks my fine ass back into gear, using both hands to yank a black blade out of Ari's back. The hole left behind quickly fills with blood, so I toss the weapon and grab one of the kitchen towels hanging off the stove rail, pressing down. Ruby blood still seeps into the cloth, so I press harder, leveraging my body weight. I hear rustling and turn to face the man who carried Ari as he studies me like I'm an animal in a zoo.

"Umm. I'm Rhys," I offer. Seems only decent.

"Drystan. You must be his little human mate. I can see why he's so twisted up about you. Stubborn demon. You can move the towel."

"What?" What does a towel have to do with me?

"The towel. He should be done bleeding." I hesitantly lift the towel and see the last of his injury knit itself up. Freaky. I glance at the black blade. The coloring looks a lot like the sphere I held a few days ago. Should I ask? Who am I kidding, of course I'll ask.

"What is it? Why didn't you remove it? What happened?" I say, gesturing to the weapon.

"Vamp got him when he was distracted or outnumbered. Not big on the details since I was busy myself. It's actually obsidian. It's a protective crystal made from lava, essentially. One of the most potent in existence, and the only thing that can really harm demons after being made into a weapon. It maintains its same strength no matter what's done to it. Salt in a weapon means nothing, not like a salt circle. It's funny, though. The most powerful healing crystal actually stops our accelerated healing if we are cut or stabbed with it.

"Anyway. Like I said, it stops our accelerated healing, making the wound inflicted near what a mortal would experience. I couldn't remove the blade—I tried. It's spelled to only be removed by a vampire . . . or a mortal, I'm assuming, because you were able to remove it." I don't share my Null status. He can stand to be confused until I talk to Ari about what I should and shouldn't be telling people.

That actually brings up a good fucking point. I can't help the glare I shoot him. "Why come here? We don't have a vampire here! He could have died!"

He gives a small nod. "The last thing he said clearly before he passed out the second time was your name and Lily's. I took a chance. If you couldn't do anything, I would have popped in and grabbed a vamp from somewhere and forced them to remove it." He shrugs like it isn't a big deal, but I saw his panic when they came through the portal.

"You're really just a softie." I smirk at him.

I can hear his answering scoff, but my eyes can't help but sweep over Ari again to make sure he's really okay and here with me. I find his beautiful grey eyes open and locked on to me. I gasp and cup his jaw, running my thumb along his cheekbone. He turns slightly and kisses it. Well, that's new.

"How are you feeling?" I murmur. I can see the stress lines have faded quite a bit from his face, but he could just be hiding it now that he's conscious.

"I'm okay, sweet Rhys. I promised to come back. It may not be how I planned, but I will always come back as long as you want me to."

"Why wouldn't I want you to come back? You're my mate." It's better for me to tell him I know all about his sneaky-sneaky now so he won't clam up and get all formal with me once he's thinking clearly. I smack his arm.

"What the hell, Ari? Why didn't you tell me before I left? I thought I was having a heart attack or I was finally cracking!" *See? Told ya I'd smack him.* Not how I intended, but I won't hurt a man recovering from a stab wound, not when I could dress in a nurse's costume and make him oh so much better.

"How do you feel about fishnets?" Jesus, my filter, where the fuck did it go?

"Do you want answers to all the questions you asked or just the last one?"

"Just the last, please. For now."

"Um, okay. They're useful. Why are we talking about fishing?"

An honest-to-God giggle slips out before I can catch it. "Like fishnet stockings. I was thinking extra naughty nurse, but if you'd rather—Eeep!"

I squeal as he turns onto his back and hauls me up onto the island on top of him, my legs straddling his thick waist. Thank God I'm not a smaller guy; my legs barely fit comfortably this way as it is. I've never had a man make me feel weightless before, and if my cock being hard enough to pound nails is any indication, I'm, like, SUPER into it.

I check on Drystan, maybe so I could catch his reaction, but the space where he was standing is empty. Where did he go? Ari pulls my face down, brushing his lips softly against mine once, twice, and again before pulling back. My thoughts about Drystan vanished the second his lips connected with mine. Why did he stop?

I chase his mouth with mine just to coerce one more out of him, but he holds my head firmly and whispers, "You're perfect." The sincerity in his eyes and the hint of awe in his voice makes my eyes water. I've never had anyone look at me the way he is right now. My heart softens even more; the tingles comfort me where our bodies touch. I know he'll push me away again, but I'll be stronger. He deserves so much more than I can give him, but I'm a greedy bitch. The concern on his face shows I'm no better at filtering my face than I am at what comes out of my mouth. Nope, not missing this. Back on track.

"Kiss me?" It comes out a little more desperately than I'd wanted, but I don't regret showing him how much I need it. His mouth crashes to mine. Our first few kisses may have been gentle caresses, but this one? I'm being consumed. He tilts my head the way he wants it, moving one hand from the side of my head to grip my hair tight enough to make me wince and my cock throb.

I surrender, loving the subtle manhandling, involuntarily rutting against him and moaning loudly into his mouth. He growls in response, tongue fucking into my mouth, leaving nothing in there untouched. His tongue seems to lengthen and curl, swirling my soft palate. Who knew that was an erogenous zone? His grip gets even tighter when no protest comes from me; maybe he's truly catching on that I'd be willing for him to tie me up and fuck me into the mattress. Yes, please.

"Fuck, Rhys. I need a minute or I'll explode in my pants like a youngling." I whimper in protest. He's stealing my breath, lips still hovering over mine. It's fine, I don't need to breathe, just need *him*. My ass actually fucking twitches because of the hint of breath play I'm experiencing right now. I feel out of control, just want him to continue to overwhelm me. I start to feel floaty but hot all over.

"Shhh, baby, I'll take care of you." He coos at me, moving the hand not tangled in my hair over my shoulder and down my back, seeking skin. He slips his hand into the back of my pants, grabbing the flesh of my cheeks and squeezing hard enough to rock me forward, rubbing my clothed cock against his again. The noises I'm making against his lips are positively obscene. I'd be embarrassed (maybe), but his dirty talk is truly on point. His voice is rough, speaking into my slack, panting mouth. He moves his head as he talks, reaching my ear. Oh God, that's definitely connected straight to my balls.

"That's it, take what you need. I'm going to own this ass, baby, such a sweet hole, so soft." His finger had found its way between my cheeks, just rubbing my soft opening.

After I relax enough, he's pushing in, just to the first knuckle since there's no lube. The shallow fucking doesn't seem like quite enough, but combined with the humping my hips are still doing—without my permission, I might add—it won't take but another few seconds. His voice is a wet dream in itself. Rasping breaths skitter over me as he leans to whisper into my ear.

"You need part of me in there, sweet Rhys?" He flicks his tongue out to trace the shell of my ear. Oh God, I'm going to explode. "It's mine, isn't it? You're *MINE*."

That's all it takes before I fall apart, white flashing behind my eyes. My body stiffens all the way to my toes as I scream his name. My orgasm seems to go on forever, his hips continuing to rub our cocks together until he grunts and comes with a deep, stuttering groan. Hands down the hottest thing I've ever experienced.

I collapse onto his chest, not caring about the mess in my pants. I realize we're still lying on the kitchen island, which cannot be comfy for Ari. I attempt to wiggle off of him, but he curls those massive arms around me and tightens them like a cuddly straight jacket. I keep my eyes closed and give in, kissing his naked chest before drifting off, trusting him to take care of me. I know I'll hate waking up with dry come everywhere down there, but that's future Rhys's problem. I feel his lips move against my neck as if he's saying something, but I can't pull myself back to awareness enough to understand.

Chapter Six

Rhys

I stare at the ceiling of the room I woke up in, arm thrown to the side of the bed that's still made, feeling the cool sheets. He didn't stay. My eyes prick at the thought. He must have cleaned me up. I don't feel sticky and I'm pretty sure I'm naked, though I haven't actually looked. A single tear slips free, and I swipe it away. May as well face the music.

The door opens, and Ari walks in with a glass of orange juice and a bowl of what looks like oatmeal. My confusion on the food choice pales compared to the joy. He didn't leave, just got breakfast. I watch him, the silence not quite comfortable, and try to think of something to say. His smile skips a fraction and the muscle in his jaw jumps.

"I brought you breakfast. I didn't know what you like. If you dislike oatmeal, I can grab you something else."

"No, oatmeal is fine. Thank you."

He gives me a tender look. "I know we have a lot to talk about, but would you indulge me and tell me about yourself while we eat? You need sugar. It might help." I groan internally. I hate giving my life story, but since I'd like to know more about him just as much, I can't avoid it.

"What would you like to know?"

"Anything you wish to share. I don't expect you to spill all your secrets; I just want to know you." He looks human. I wonder if it takes energy staying that way or if it's more comfortable. I'll have to ask later. Yay for a functioning filter!

I accept the offered bowl and take a bite, stalling to gather my thoughts again. I swallow the sweetened oats, tasting blueberries. "Well, I'm twenty-four, work at a go-go dance club closer to downtown. I'm a cat person but honestly love animals in general . . . except spiders. Those things are creepy as fuck." I keep my gaze down, gathering courage to talk about more than the relationship version of the weather.

"No spiders, I can work with that. What do you do at the club?" I can see he struggled with the last part. Why? I think about what I said and realized he probably thinks I'm a dancer. Jokes on him.

I chuckle. "I'm a bartender. I'm not pretty enough to dance. I have okay coordination, but most dancers fall into twink or gym rat categories. Soft bodies don't come in first for a lot of people's preferred body type for dancers. If I had to put myself into a category, it'd be a dad bod, or an otter. I'm too big to be a real twink. Now cuddling? I'm a pro."

His scowl started around the first sentence but looks deadly by the time I cut off my rambling. "You're perfect. Not pretty enough? Rhys, you're gorgeous. If I have to tell you daily until you see what I see, I can do that. Why do you believe you're too big to be a twink? I'm not one hundred percent certain on these categorizations, but you seem to think the only thing putting you into another category is your size. You're the perfect size. Small enough to haul around but not so small that I'd break you if I squeezed a tad too hard."

My chest warms. "You're not exactly a normal human size, Ari. You're giant." I would feel like a child, but I could probably comfortably sit on his hip like I've seen toddlers do to their moms.

He grumbles but doesn't contradict me. "Cats or dogs?" I ask just to distract him from trying to convince me I shit rainbows. My courage about telling him more faded right around when the compliments started. I haven't had anyone think I'm worth anything in so long; I'd like to keep it just a little longer.

His beautiful eyes turn sad. Does my preference on pets really carry this much weight? I might be overthinking this, but I have to answer honestly. "Well, I cannot say I prefer either way. I have not spent an adequate amount of time with anything a human would call their pet. We have animal-like things in Hell, but they're made of smoke and shadows, really. I grew to care for a fire shadowling when I was young. Not particularly affectionate like I've heard pets are, but it was good company when I didn't want to feel lonely." I feel like a tool when I start talking like I'm from Old England, but it's a default from when I was trained to be among humans. I don't want to come off as a brute or a lunatic, so I temper myself when I can.

"Shadowlings, what do they look like?" He actually looks eager. I latch on, glad to have a way to entertain him. Not many of my stories are particularly good ones—even this one is kind of twisty. "Like the shadow they're named after. They leave an impression when they touch the ground, but most times they hover. Like smoke. Their form changes, moving almost constantly. They represent each element: air, fire, earth, water. They keep a balance of sorts in Hell."

He motions for me to go on. "Shadowlings are what become of certain low-level demons when they pass a final time. Since no living thing can survive Hell unless they're a demon or angel, shadowlings provide the elements. No plants lead to no air, so the air shadowlings provide them. Hell owns a soul after the person passes. The soul is gifted their demon form as a way to live again until their final death. Since Hell already owns that soul, they cannot re-enter Hell as a demon. Instead, the soul's energy sustains Hell within the shadows. The shadowling's age starts over at transformation, kind of like vampires."

His fascinated gaze never leaves me. "Is there anything else about my home you'd like to know?" I know I'm giving him an easy out for answering questions about his own life, but I want to prolong the look on his face now. It's like a dam bursts. He throws ten questions at me in rapid succession. I struggle to keep them all straight in my head, but I'm becoming better at it. This seems to be a habit of his, and I find it endearing. I answer as best I can, filling in gaps about how Hell is run, the basics of my team, what makes demons different from each other. My team house brings another onslaught of questions, but his eyes are growing heavy. I look at the clock and realize we talked straight through lunch.

"Sweet Rhys, I promise I will answer your questions, but we need to grab more food. And although I would love to nap with you after chatting some more, Lily told me you have a weapons session with her this afternoon."

"Ugh! Don't remind me. I'm terrible at wielding anything bigger than a pen." His pout calls for me to kiss it away. I can't resist swooping down for a taste before we head to grab food. As I stand from the bed, I look back and catch the small smile on his lips, his blush almost reaching his ears. So sweet. I busy myself in the bathroom while he gets dressed. I'd love to watch him, but seeing his body encased in pretty pale-purple briefs last night was hard enough. Wiping him down and undressing him at my leisure was a sweet torture. His toenails matched his underwear, and I've never thought about that as sexy before but I sure as fuck do now.

We walk hand in hand to the kitchen, my cock twitching again as we pass the island. I leave him at the barstools and go digging in the fridge. The flash of submission I saw in him last night makes it hard to focus, my mind replaying on a loop the moment he gave in to me. My mate snickers, reminding me of my task. Wrath wriggles, pushing me to feed my mate.

I don't know how the others think of their sin side, but Wrath is almost like a separate entity. He has always been pushy, contradicting my want for organization. I like control in all aspects, whereas he revels in chaos. Apparently taking care of our mate is something we can agree on. He was never as involved with Liam, taking a backseat happily. Wrath wanting to nurture our mate instead of ignore him throws me. I hadn't noticed how in sync we'd been for the most part. Only when I tried to create distance with Rhys has he pushed for the driver's seat. Otherwise, he has been a content passenger, intrigued by Rhys's physicality but also enjoying just letting him talk. This symbiotic relationship has always been a tug of war. Rhys settles something in both of us, giving a common goal we want to put above all others.

Rhys's movement out of the corner of my eye pulls me out of my introspection. Right, food. At least my erection isn't a problem anymore. I gather everything to make quick sandwiches. Putting them together gives me enough time to gather the courage to ask Wrath's question. His deep desire to really meet our mate.

"I must confess something, mate. I explained my relationship to my sin as best I could at the time, but I . . . okay, we . . . we feel like I didn't do it justice. Wrath would like to properly meet you." His eyes widen to saucers and my heart stutters, terrified he won't accept all of me.

"He's that sentient? I can meet him?! Was that him I saw when you changed before?" He bounces in his seat, shoving a bite in his mouth, no doubt stemming the flow of questions he wants to ask.

"Kind of? I like to think of him that way. He's as much a part of me as a shifter and their animal. His instincts aren't as basic; he embodies the 'wrath' portion of me so I can function normally day to day." I sigh, not knowing how to describe my relationship to Wrath; I've never had to before.

"We don't communicate like you and I do. More akin to feelings and urges he can push at me. The only time he can truly take over is with my consent or in extreme danger. Although he really doesn't have a moral compass, he asks to 'be in the driver's seat' so rarely that I usually comply as long as there aren't innocents around." Oh! "And no, last time was still me." I rush to clarify. "Not that he would hurt you, I don't think. You intrigue him."

"Like a science experiment?" His face falls like he's disappointed.

"I don't think so. He's a little disgusted at how I'm bungling this, actually. He doesn't use speech to communicate normally, maybe a word here or there, so I'm not sure how he will try to do so with you. He's rather insistent that he do it himself, though. Maybe we can try after dinner? I have to update my team while you train. Is that okay?" What if he is scared? "I understand—"

"Of course! Can I meet your team?" I do a double take at his eager expression. There is no fear to be found. Wait.

"My team? Why?"

"Well, I've already kind of met Drystan. I'd like to meet your friends, if that's okay?" His eyes cast downward, and his knuckles clench on his plate. His nerves tickle in my chest.

"They're not really my friends. I'd say I'm closer to Drys, but they're my team. Close by necessity."

"So you don't hang out outside of work? You all live together."

"Not really. Maybe the occasional text in the group, but it's mostly work related." He seems saddened by my admission. I panic and blurt, "You can meet them!" before I can think about it. I don't really want the other demons close to him, especially Kieran, but Wrath seems to be brushing away my concerns.

"Really? Yessss!" He pumps his fist like he's celebrating a great victory. I concede to the feeling that I would do anything to make my human happy. We haven't broached the subject of completing our mate bond, but I find myself not dreading it anymore. I won't rush this, but I won't put off the conversation if he brings it up.

Chapter Seven

Rhys

My heart hammers in my chest. Why did I think this was a good idea? What if they all hate me? I'd feel terrible messing up their mojo during an assignment. I try to get my head straight so I can focus on Lily, but it's impossible.

"You're going to be fine, Rhys. They'll love you. You're safe; Ari will rip them apart before he lets them hurt you." She pats my arm like that's somehow reassuring. That is precisely why I'm freaking out. My filter must be holding pretty strong for me not to say anything crazy.

"Deep breaths, baby." Arms wrap around my waist from behind. I do as Ari says and breathe, letting my head drop back onto his chest. It might be an overused nickname, but him calling me baby is just chef's kiss. I sigh as my heart rate slows and I feel better. I spin around and snuggle into his firm pecs.

"How did you know I was spazzing?"

His eyes crinkle with mirth. "I can feel you panicking."

"You can feel that?" I thought it just hurt when we weren't together. I have so many questions. I know he can either tell by my face or feel it through the bond that isn't there yet, because his small smile widens and he gets a tender look in his eye.

"Well now, how precious." I startle a bit, trying to find the source of the voice. I blank on a name—well, because I haven't seen any of their faces—but this must be someone from Ari's team. Black hair, blue eyes, pale as all get out, tattoos covering both arms, and some cheekbones I'd cut a bitch for. He's bigger than I am but not even close to Ari or Drystan's size. I try to give a welcoming smile.

"Devland, this is Rhys." Ari almost growls out the introduction, not letting me go completely, tucking me into his side. I hold out my hand to shake his. No idea why I thought that'd be the thing to do, but I'm fucking nervous. He gives me a smirk that borders on a sneer and shakes my hand, putting a lot of pressure on my knuckles. Ari stiffens beside me, and I can feel Wrath pushing angrily under his skin. Whoa, that's a weird-as-fuck sensation. I shiver, and both demons notice. Devland's eyes spark with interest, but Ari gives me a slight frown. I drop Devland's hand like a hot potato. Both must have misunderstood my shiver, but I don't have time to explain my reaction to Ari.

A boy glides into the room, and I immediately know who he is. He's a perfect mix of feminine and masculine features, dainty but strong. I know he has to be older than I am; he's around my size, but he looks young. Twenty, maybe? Innocence wrapped in sex. This has to be the lust demon. I'm not affected by the magic he gives off, but I can actually feel it like a hovering caress, sliding over me but not actually touching. So weird. His skin is deeply tanned, culturally ambiguous, but I would imagine all demons are to a point. His eyes are copper, almost like the tiger's eye stone I saw in Lily's shop. He gives me a sweet seductive smile and tosses his long dark-blond hair over his shoulder. He doesn't speak, just waits. I don't know what he's waiting for, but I cannot stand the silence.

"Hey, I'm Rhys." I put out my hand again; hopefully it won't get crushed this time. His smile falters for a second.

"He won't touch you, baby, not unless we can prove for sure he won't affect you. Let's try talking first."

Umm, okay?

"You're Kieran, right? The lust demon? It makes sense; you're, like, really pretty. Oh God, I didn't mean to quote *Mean Girls*. That's awful and a tacky-gay move. I'm not usually a tacky gay. You can wear pink whenever you want, not that you have to. It's not a Wednesday-only deal. You're wearing white. It's a good color but makes people think you're a virgin and they should help you. Is that why you wear it? Have you tried mustard yellow? I can't think that that color would be flattering with your skin tone and hair, but then again, you're bound to pull off anything. Maybe a parka? It'd cover that banging body, though, and that's a fucking crime. I'd flaunt the shit out of that ass, too, if I had it. Mine's not bad, just a little big, and oh my God why won't I stop talking?!" Finally, Ari's giant hand covers my mouth, and I sag in relief and just a little (lotta) bit of humiliation. Ari chuckles behind me and Kieran giggles. It sounds like tinkling bells. Ari kisses my temple, and I relax a little more.

"Hi, Rhys. That was quite an introduction." He waits a beat. "How do you feel right now?"

"Embarrassed? Like I would swan dive into a lake of spiders to avoid rambling like that again?" If my filter is this broken, I can't imagine how it'll be when the others get here.

Ari reassures the demons by affirming I'm a rambler and talk faster than my brain can think. I want to be offended, but it's true and I dislike lying, even to myself. Drystan walks in next, surveying the room. I capitalize on his ignorance that I just made an ass out of myself and jog over to him.

"Drystan! How are you doing? Can I get you anything?" I give him some pretty serious "help me" eyes, but he just pats my head and ignores them. Slinging his arm around my shoulders, he turns us to the little trio and starts walking me back over.

"I'm just fine, Rhys. How are you? No out-of-control feeling? Want to jump on Kieran's dick or hump his leg?" Ohhhh. Is it because he's a lust demon?

"He's, like, stupid hot, but all of you are. I'm fine. Is that what this was about?" I look to Ari for confirmation. He's frowning a touch. Oh shit, I did just say his team was hot.

"We needed to make sure you didn't get crazy and try to kill or fuck everyone in the room. It'd get some of us laid out or worse if the wrath demon took offense," Devland explains quickly. It makes sense so I just nod.

"So I pass?" Still looking at Ari, I don't miss the flash in his eyes, and I realize Drystan still has his arm around me. I shrug it off and reach for Ari. I'm immediately tucked back into his side as he grumbles and runs his hand over my shoulder, smoothing out my shirt with one hand. I kiss him wherever is closest, practically his armpit, but it seems to mollify him.

The rest of the group files in, and I understand their need to test me first. Introductions fly and I think I talk back, though I have no idea what I said. I just can't stop staring. There are so many of them. Magic slides all over my skin. I'm aware it's there, but I don't feel different. I am extremely drawn to Belial, the kind of pull I felt with Ari but nothing stirs below my chest. Just an extra layer of warmth. I haven't spoken to him yet, but I know who he is by default. He hangs back so far from everyone that he's almost not in the room. I can't stop staring, and I feel like I'm being rude but I need to touch him.

I weave my way around the team and wrap my arms around his waist. His startled look almost hurts, like he's never been hugged before. I hear a roar behind me and look over my shoulder. Wrath is visible in Ari's eyes, his skin rippling like waves.

"Wrath, hush. Come here." I attempt to soothe him. His demon form now fully out, he stalks toward me. The room has given Ari a wide berth, so there's no one between us. I don't let go of Belial, though he tries to tug me off of him. I don't quite understand what's happening, but Ari/Wrath needs to help me.

"What is Belial again? Envy demon, right?" He stills a few feet away, skin rippling again like Ari is fighting for control. That settles that. I won't be letting go of the demon I'm attached to until I'm sure I won't be causing his death today.

He gives a stiff nod and takes another jerky step forward. I grab Wrath's wrist once he's close enough, pulling his clawed hand onto my chest.

"I feel something right here. It's not envy, nothing negative. It's like our bond but not. I don't want to fuck him, just hug him. Like a brother, or like I would with Sasha, maybe deeper? What does it mean?"

Wrath's face says he still *really* doesn't like me touching another demon, but he isn't ripping anyone apart yet, so I'm calling it a win. I can feel Belial starting to breathe again, so maybe he also sees that his life isn't so much on the line anymore. I slowly disengage, giving up my koala status but remaining between them. Wrath seems to accept what I'm saying, giving Ari back the driver's seat. I don't want to chance moving away from Belial quite yet.

"Get Lily!" he barks at Kek. With a roll of his violet eyes, Kek struts back out of the room. We wait in tense silence, and I realize outside of introductions, I haven't heard Belial talk. I half-turn to him so I can see both demons.

"Are you okay? I'm sorry if I made you mad by hugging you . . . and not letting go. I figured it was better if you weren't standing alone anymore." He gives me a soft smile and nods. I want to hug him again but stop myself.

"What do you need, Aridam?! Why was I dragged away? You cannot summon me like a child." She's feeling extra prickly, probably because her place is full of demons she didn't ask for.

"Is there a bond between Rhys and Belial? If so, what is it?"

"Oh! Well, let's take a look." She stares at my chest and follows something no one else can see and stares at Belial. Her face twitches, and she rushes out the word "twin" before fleeing the room. What the hell?

Belial's eyes turn sad as he watches her go, but then he turns to me and they clear a bit. "She said twin souls. It's like soulmates but platonic, the perfect support match to make us a whole person."

Oh, that's cool! "Can you feel my emotions like Ari can?"

"No, Rhys. It's just a sense of peace. That's what I get from you. Peace and warmth." His gaze holds mine, reverence in their emerald-green depths.

I know when Ari told me about Belial, his words were tinged with regret and sorrow. Belial's control is broken; he affects anyone near him. Kind of like Kieran's lust mojo, but Bel's is more dangerous, quicker. He constantly infects everyone around him with envy. Not just mortals. Not only does he not have an off switch, he's always on high. Even his team can't spend too much time with him before they feel the effects and get a little crazy.

"As touching as this is, could we maybe get a move on? We have a job to do that's more important than Belial's sudden ability to not be murdered within five minutes of touching a person," Azvameth drawls from across the room, leaning unbothered on the frame of the doorway.

Kek smacks the back of his head to shush him. I can't help but watch Kek. His ebony skin is a startling backdrop to those light-purple eyes. They give him an otherworldly appearance, which I guess is completely accurate. The grin he flashes me looks like a feral snarl.

Ari sighs but admits Az has a point. "We will discuss this later." His eyes bore into me, telling me without words he is going crazy wanting to stake his claim. Good. I hate that we aren't bonded. It's been a crazy week, but my life has been crazy from the get go. At least this kind of crazy comes with a soulmate—someone in my corner forever. Someone to choose me.

I know Ari is getting the short end of the stick. He'll want to trade me in for a new mate eventually, but I want to soak up what I can while I can. I need memories to treasure after he leaves me behind. I try to force a smile for him, but I definitely missed the mark if his raised eyebrow is any indication.

We filter into a meeting room Lily usually reserves for séances and chakra adjustments. It's a tight fit with the eight of us, so Ari squeezes me into his lap to give them more space. I snort out loud but ignore the looks. He probably just wants me to be as close as possible while

Bel is in the room. I wiggle around to get comfy as they start to discuss strategies.

They each give Ari their reports, giving us a bigger picture as to what might be happening to the missing souls. At the center are Constantine and his coven. He's actively culling supernaturals for their blood. Gives him and his coven a leg up, and he's expanding his territory at an alarming rate.

"There's no answer as to why the souls aren't showing at Reception like they're supposed to. The first name on the list showed up almost six months after its intended arrival, soul torn to shreds. I've never seen anything like it." Drystan's face is carefully blank, but he can't hide the anger in his voice.

"There has to be a pattern, but so far we can't find it," Kek chips in. This time, the smugness is absent from his tone.

"We've come up with a decent plan for tonight. We need a break and to come back in the morning to hammer out the details. Our window to recover the last few names is getting smaller, but we cannot go in halfcocked again. Now that we know they're like vamps on steroids, we need a different approach. Using brute force won't work with their numbers this time. Think on it. We'll reconvene at eight." Ari seems to end the meeting just like that.

They all stand, except for Bel. He once again hasn't spoken unless absolutely necessary and had pulled back from the table, almost to the corner of the room. He calmly waits until it's just us three before speaking. "I know you're unhappy, Aridam. We can figure this all out after we take out Constantine. I promise to not interfere or get too close to Rhys if he could just hang out in the command center with me for a little bit sometimes."

You can hear the loneliness; it's a physical thing surrounding him like a dark cloud. My eyes prick at the thought of him continuing to feel like this when I could help. Ari nods but doesn't say anything. I elbow his ribs none too gently, and he huffs. "You don't have to avoid Rhys, Bel. Just give me some time to get Wrath to understand. If you were to hug him again right now, I don't know that I could stop him from killing you."

Bel dips his head, and I smile and wave at him. He walks out the door without looking back, shoulders slumped, almost caving in on himself. I'll cuddle the shit out of him once I get my grumpy demon in line.

"Okay, meeting over. Lemme meet him all proper-like."

"Give me a minute, baby. He's still upset about Belial."

"No. Now. I can explain it to him just like you can. He's my demon too. Stop being stingy."

Ari chuckles like I'm kidding, but leans back and gently pushes the chair away from the table, letting me continue to straddle him. "He wants to solidify our bond, Rhys. He'll be extremely pushy, but if you tell him he'll hurt you by doing it against your will, he'll back off."

My chest twinges in concern. "So he wants to bond with me but you don't?" I need to know.

"What? No! I mean, yes, of course I want to bond with you. It will be a pretty big change for you, though. Your lifespan will match mine"—my heart hammers. I won't have to leave him because of old age? Thank God—"and it'll be harder to kill you, but not impossible. Our lifespans aren't tied; if I die, it won't kill you, but the bond breaking might." I nod and motion for him to continue.

"We'll be able to feel each other's emotions better than now. Like a constant trickle of vague information, with gushes when the emotion is extreme, from what I've heard. No two bonds are exactly the same, but it's common for wrath demons to filter out that layer of them that's always angry. You will be one hundred percent mine, sweet Rhys. I won't be able to handle you touching another demon, won't allow you to leave. Are you sure you want this? Me? Us?"

I don't have to wait, don't need the out he's trying to give me. "Yes. Make me yours, but first, let me talk to Wrath."

Joy bursts through my chest. I know it's coming from Ari, even as he leans back and closes his eyes. When he opens them, they've gone liquid metal and the lap I'm sitting on is a bit bigger than before. His horns are right the fuck there, so I lean in and stroke a finger up the front of one. His body shudders, and he grunts.

"Mate." His growl is like gravel, so low and throaty. His nose skims across my cheek, sliding down behind my ear where he leaves an open mouth kiss. He drags his mouth down to the juncture between my neck and shoulder, fangs skimming my skin there, not drawing blood but bringing it to the surface. I can't help but moan.

"Mate." He breathes it, almost like a prayer. He grabs my hips, squeezing to the point of pain. He continues to breathe in my scent, nuzzling there. A rumble in his chest makes it seem like he's purring.

"Hi, Wrath." I have to start somewhere, so I whisper it while running my hands up his powerful shoulders, fingers playing with the hair at the nape of his neck. "You have to talk to me, big guy. Are you okay?"

"Mine!" he rasps out against my shoulder.

"Yours. You wanna keep me? I don't think I can handle Ari giving me up and finding another mate right now, Wrath. You have to be sure. No takesies-backsies here."

"Stay. Mine. Safe." My skin tingles where his lips touch me.

"You gonna keep me safe?" He grunts and nods his head. "Look at me, big guy. I wanna see those pretty eyes." He leans back immediately, silver eyes framed by the longest lashes, looking so earnest. His vocabulary is lacking, but his grunted words melt me. The demon that legit represents all righteous fury and angry chaos is gentle with me. It's a heady feeling. A little bruising from his grip doesn't scare me; my raging hard on hasn't faltered once.

"Rhys, stay. Mate?" Seems almost like a question. It might not be, but I'll answer him anyway.

"Yeah, Wrath, I'll be yours and his. You just have to give me Ari back so we can get to that part, okay? I wanted to spend some time with you so we could meet. I know we'll be mated, too, in a way. I know you won't be in the driver's seat often, but is that okay?"

"Aridam . . . me. Both Ari. I keep safe. He feed mate."

I chuckle and kiss his nose. "Okay, then let's do this thing. I'm getting hungry again."

Wow, he must really hate the idea of me being hungry. I'm still sitting on his lap, so when his eyes stop swirling, I know I have Ari back. He lets go of his demon form, standing with an arm under my ass, and brings my leg to wrap around his waist. I help as much as I can by doing a magnificent spider monkey impression. I thought maybe we would talk a little more, but it seems like that time has passed.

"I need you, sweet Rhys." He lowers his lips, devouring me. I hope he doesn't run into anything, but I can't think anymore. His mouth is too hot; the slide of his tongue against mine is all I can focus on.

Chapter Eight

Aridam

I navigate us as best I can, not stopping until my knees hit the bed of the room we woke up in this morning. I need to taste him. I reluctantly pull my mouth away. Whipping his shirt off and dropping him on the bed, I watch my mate bounce slightly. He's so beautiful, all flushed with arousal, pupils blown wide. It's hard to form words, but I manage to grunt out my request for him to be naked, grabbing at the waistband of his pants.

"I want to see you too." His tone pleading, like I could deny him a damned thing. I unceremoniously pull off my shirt and throw it on the floor to join his. The pants I'm wearing are stretchy, so I pull down both pants and briefs together. I kick them aside and bend down to quickly remove my socks, thanking past me for not putting on boots that take forever to lace. I freeze when I look up again. Rhys is spread out on the bed, his chest down against the sheets, ass in the air. It's the hottest thing I've ever seen. I spot his hand sneaking down to grab his length, giving a few slow pulls. My mouth waters. I give myself a stroke for some relief; the small ridges along my shaft pulse with need. I don't waste another second before I'm on him, flipping him onto his back.

"I don't know if I can be gentle this time, sweet Rhys. I need you. Need to feel you around me." His moan is answer enough. I reach to the nightstand drawer and grab the lube that's been stashed there since this morning, thanks to Lily. I toss it down next to my knee, pulling his legs up to rest on my hips. I can't resist bending down and licking his pretty pink nipples, giving them equal attention as I pick the bottle back up and coat my fingers. He whimpers and arches against my touch; those needy sounds push at me. I need more. Dragging my finger down his weeping cock, I don't do more than lightly touch, knowing he could go off at any time.

"Wait for me, baby; I need to feel you fall apart on my dick."

"So good, Ari . . . please, please."

His words become a chant as my fingers rub and pull on the edges of his dusty pink hole, waiting for that tight ring to soften just a little more. I push in a single finger, sliding it into his tight heat, waiting for him to get used to the stretch. His begging intensifies, and he gives a throaty groan as I add a second. If I don't get him stretched, neither of us will make it.

"Ari! Close!"

I quickly grab the base of his cock to stave off the orgasm getting ready to rush through him. I quickly add a third finger with the help of more lube, barely waiting for him to adjust before I push in another. The burn of four seems to have given him enough of a distraction that I'm not worried about him coming, at least for a little bit.

"Good boy, this tight little hole is going to let me in, take all of it." His body is made for me, so sweet and pliable in my hands. He's finally ready. My mate gives a strangled cry as I shove into him. The grip his ass has on my cock is borderline painful. Head thrown back, mouth open, fists tangled in the sheets below him. He's perfect. It's all I can do to stay still.

I finally give in to my urge to thrust and can't censor myself. "Oh baby, so hot, so tight. You feel perfect, so perfect for me." His sweet noises are out of control, like a mewling kitten. I fuck into him harder and faster, long strokes so I bottom out each time. The ridges catch on his rim and prostate with each thrust. I won't be able to hold back much longer, but I need him to come first. "Wanna feel you come on my cock. Need to fill you up, mark you as mine. Come for me; show me how good it feels." I reach for his length, letting one leg go. My hand is covered in the pre-come that's been flowing from him since we started. With one firm stroke, he falls apart. Shooting hard, back bowing completely off the bed. I feel him spasm around me, pushing me over the edge.

I lean forward and gather his body to mine on autopilot, our orgasms starting to wane, and lick the spot I'll be

claiming on his neck. Fangs spring from my mouth as I
call on my demon form once again. His hole stretches
impossibly wide over my new girth, and he writhes in my
arms, crying out at the new sensation of the more defined
ridges and larger girth. My tail has a mind of its own,
wrapping around his still-hard length as my wings curl
around his back, cocooning us. I strike, biting down.
Something in my chest snaps into place, and my cock
gives another spurt as a new wave of pleasure runs
through us, melding with the first. My stomach is covered
in his essence, growing cold, but I can't feel anything but
content. Wrath purrs in my chest, and our bond to our
mate hums. I finish licking the scarring bite I left behind,
loving the little shivers running through Rhys with every
touch to his mark. He looks beautifully wrecked, giving
me the sweetest little smile, pursing his reddened lips for
a kiss. I can't help but to oblige. This little human is my
everything. He can have anything he wants; he just has to
ask.

I slowly take my human form again, my come running
around my softening cock and down his thighs. His eyes
barely flutter. I pull back my wings and gently place him
on the clean side of the bed, grabbing my discarded shirt
to clean us up as best I can. I pull the dirty sheets off the
bed, moving him when needed. Through all my
ministrations, he doesn't stir. I climb in next to him and
cover us with the blanket. Pushing aside the hair that has
plastered to his face, I just watch him. This is what
mating is supposed to feel like. After a long while of

studying him in his sleep, I curl possessively around my mate, closing my eyes to enjoy the feel of him in my arms.

- - -

Light sneaking through the window has me snapping my eyes open. It's usually impossible for me to sleep anywhere but home, especially in my more vulnerable body. With Rhys next to us, apparently Wrath can calm down enough to let me get some shut-eye.

Sweet Rhys. I feel the weight of him against my side, head on my chest and leg draped over mine. He moved quite a bit in his sleep, but the bond seems peaceful, just active enough to feel like he's been dreaming. He has a single hand resting on my abdomen right under the piercing he seems to be fascinated with. I can't help but trace the outline of his long fingers. His skin is so soft on top, a direct opposite from the callouses and roughness gained by hard labor on his palms. His breathing changes, and I know he's waking up, his soft lips parting in surprise. I give him a minute so he can catch up.

"When is the meeting?" His voice is heavy with sleep. Only one question? He must need to fully wake up before his brain is firing on all cylinders.

"We have some time." It won't start without us. The team will arrive soon, but I don't want to rush him.

"Coffee, Ari. It's calling my name." He sits up, obviously still gathering himself enough to leave the bed. I wish we could stay wrapped around each other all day. I watch his back bunch as he pushes himself off the bed, giving me an unencumbered view of his bitable ass. My dick perks up.

He scowls at me over his shoulder. "None of that. We have things to do, and I'm just slutty enough to let you take me back to bed even when my ass is still on fire from last night. No. No more 'I'm going to fuck you until you scream' eyes, got it? I can feel your arousal; it's distracting. I can't pee with a hard on!"

I smirk. "I make no apologies. My mate is incredibly sexy. You don't know what you do to me, sweet Rhys." I know the nickname pushes all his buttons. One or two carefully placed words and my mate turns into submissive putty in my hands. I won't push; we do have things to do, but I can't let him think I'm not ready to push inside of his hot little body anytime, anywhere.

He doesn't realize I can see his soft smile. Wrath wriggles in my mind, pushing for us to take care of our mate. I don't have time to treasure him as he deserves, though, not now. I sigh deeply, grumbling as I get up and follow him to the bathroom. Being in charge sucks sometimes, and this is definitely one of those times.

We brush our teeth, getting ready as quickly as we can while stopping frequently to give each other small touches. I head out of the room first, at my limit. Any longer and we would have ended up back in bed. Wrath doesn't seem to see the problem with that, annoyed with me for not satisfying my mate right then. I shake off the feeling, promising to fix it later.

As the team assembles in the same room as last night, I look around for Rhys and Lily. The former because I don't like the admittedly small amount of time I've been without him, and the latter because we seem to have run her out of her own space. Once we're all settled, the ribbing starts.

"Wow, Aridam, I never thought I'd see the day you let a small human lead you around. How the mighty have fallen." Kek's comment is only softened by the look in his eye. I know he likes what he's seen of Rhys so far, but I doubt his pride will let him admit he badly wants his own mate.

Another minute of good-natured teasing stops when Rhys joins us at the table, sliding into the seat I saved for him next to me. I want to pull him into my lap, but I don't know how that would be received in front of others. He looks up at me with a bit of confusion but stands again, climbing onto my lap, making himself comfortable. My cock hardens against his ass, but he does his best to ignore it. I clamp a hand on his thigh to stop his wiggling, and a giggle slips out of him. It's the best sound I've ever heard aside from the ones he makes in the bedroom. I need to hear it daily, need to make him that happy. Wrath purrs in agreement, and I know the others hear it; the chuckles from around the table are proof enough.

"So where are we at?" Rhys is apparently running this meeting, and I have no urge to take over. Our plan A is simple. Follow up on each property connected to Constantine, gather evidence on the souls, and portal back here before anyone figures out we were even there. There are a million problems with the plan, but we have yet to come up with better. I listen to ideas, vetoing some quickly while setting aside others to mull over. Devland and Kek argue the merits of splitting into teams of two versus the three Kieran and Drystan usually favor. We're fairly certain he's keeping all the souls together, but we have to have a way to split up and take any we find to Reception before coming back if we're proven wrong.

Belial is silent as usual, hanging back as much as possible, clicking away on his laptop. I don't feel any effects from his envy, but I can tell others are starting to get snappy. He's hunched in on himself, trying to appear small. Rhys notices, and through the bond, I feel the sadness and pain he feels for his new friend. I have a theory about the pair, but I am reluctant to share. I don't like sharing Rhys at all, but this might be good for both of them.

I lean in and whisper to my mate, "Go ahead, sweet Rhys; I want to see what happens when you're close to him for a while. You're dying to comfort him; I can feel it." I gently lift him from my lap, turning back to the conversation. I keep an eye on him, still listening to the team as they settle on one team of three and one of two, with Bel and one other here at Lily's.

Rhys sits next to Belial, placing a hand on his arm and leaning in to whisper. I can't hear what they're saying, but Belial seems nervous. Going by the determined set of Rhys's jaw, I'd bet he gets his way. I know I'm right when Rhys sets his hands on his hips, showing he's being extra sassy. He suddenly pushes Belial's chair back enough for him to climb onto his lap and hug him. Bel's hands go up in a placating gesture, his eyes pleading with me to not rip his head off. I know how stubborn Rhys can be, and though I really don't like the sight of my mate on someone else's lap, I know there's nothing there but friendship. I give him a small nod, letting him know that I'm aware and not upset with him. Wrath isn't even paying attention, more focused on the plans the team is setting up.

The longer Rhys clings to Belial, the more the tension in the room eases. His Null ability counteracts Bel's envy, and the team starts to notice. With a quick glance at each of us, Drystan reaches over and pulls the Bel-Rhys chair over to sit closer to the table. Rhys faces me, winking. Belial leans in and thanks him, eyes sparkling for the first time in what feels like forever. I'm so proud of my little mate.

Devland refocuses us, announcing that we have our plan for recon. Summarizing for everyone, he makes it seem like uneven teams are normal. I don't know if that's for Rhys's benefit or not, but I appreciate it. The extra team member with Bel and Rhys during these trips will rotate, giving each demon time to hang back or train with my mate. Some will be able to help in combat, others in supe history. We need to get my mate up to speed as fast as possible so we can leave him with Bel alone when we're done with recon and move on to phase two. I doubt we'll find any souls outside of the main estate, but who knows.

Chapter Nine

Rhys

"Anything?" I ask Belial as he shuts down his laptop for the day.

"Nah, we didn't really expect much from today's properties. It's why we were able to send both teams in opposite directions, though Aridam could probably do one by himself and cover a third location." He gives a small chuckle.

"I haven't seen Wrath in action yet. Is it as crazy as I imagine?"

"Probably more so. When Aridam goes feral, it's up to us to just stay out of his way. Even Drystan just lets him be. We're thankful he has as good control as he does."

I look at our companion for the day. Azvameth didn't interact with us a lot, and I find myself curious. He doesn't seem lazy like I would think a sloth demon would be. Granted, he hasn't moved from his chair all day, so maybe I'm wrong.

"Just ask, human." His voice is soft, almost bored.

"What is a sloth demon, exactly? Like, wrath and envy are pretty obvious. Sloth is confusing. What does it feel like for you? How do you affect people?"

"You know that boredom you feel when people ask unnecessary questions? That restless feeling when you're suffering through a conversation you'd rather not be having? Apathy at someone when you feel like they kind of deserve what's happening to them? That." He pauses, scowling at me. "We done here, Bel?" Without waiting for an answer, he stands and walks from the room. I can't help but feel his comments were particularly pointed.

"Oh God, he hates me!" I cry, looking at Bel.

"He doesn't hate you; he's like that with everyone."

"He's not!"

"Rhys, when have you seen him talk?"

I wrack my brain. "Umm, I don't know that I've heard him speak more than a few sentences, really."

"He just doesn't care about much. He doesn't hate you, Rhys. He's perpetually bored."

"That must suck some serious donkey balls. Hmmm, we should cheer him up. What does he like?"
"I can't tell you. He'd kill me."

"Okay, I'll just ask Ari when he gets back."

"He won't know, Rhys. I only know because I had to retrieve him once from his spot. He was ignoring the boss's summons."

I'm immediately sidetracked. "Wait, you can do that? Just ignore a Duke of Hell?"

"He's our leader, not a tyrant. I mean, he probably could be, but he's a beloved duke because he doesn't treat us like mindless drones. The rest of the team adores him. Only Az pulls shit like that when he's feeling rebellious."

"So a lot?"

Bel snorts. "Yeah, Rhys, it's his cross to bear."

I spot team one walking into the kitchen, and I rush to serve lunch. We had talked to Lily earlier this week, and she offered to go see a cousin in Ohio at her old coven so we could stay here and make this our base. She's been extremely helpful, but constantly being around all the demons and their leaking mess must have been awful for her.

"We need to send Lily a thank-you gift," I announce to the guys as they sit to devour what I made. I get a mixed bag of reactions. Kieran and Drystan look surprised, while Kek looks annoyed at my declaration.

"She should be thankful we picked her subpar shop to operate out of. With all the energy flowing through here, her sales have been crazy high."

"You're just mad because you had to man the register for a second while her staff threw themselves at Kieran. Rhys sent everyone home after that and has been the one taking care of the shop and the employees since then. It really only ruffled your feathers 'cause you weren't the prettiest in the room with him around!" Drystan loves poking at Kek. You can tell it really gets under his skin, even if he's trying his damnedest to hide it. His eyes swirl like a galaxy, all purples and blues, before settling back to their normal violet hue.

"Shhh, it's okay, Kek; you know he's just teasing." Kieran pats his hand fondly, an almost tender look in his eye. Kek's shoulders soften a fraction.

"I'll see you later, human. Tomorrow I'll be with you and Bel. I'm taking over your hand-to-hand practice, so make sure to be ready. No dallying." He's abrupt with me, leaving the table and his dirty dishes behind.

Kieran picks up his plate, taking it to the sink. "He's really not that bad. He struggles just as much with his sin as we do. Drystan, it'd be nice if you cut him some slack."

"I was kidding, Kieran. He's always so uptight. I want him to be able to loosen up a little," he says.

"Maybe leave that to Azvameth or me. Your meditation and New Age Yoga aren't really his idea of fun." Kieran lessens the blow to his newfangled habits with a quick wink and a head pat as he passes Drystan, having finished the dishes from his and Kek's lunch. He disappears into the hall. I don't know if he went to check in on Bel or if he's headed home. Not all members stay here at night.

Over the past few days, I've gotten to see the dynamics of the team, and as much as Ari denies that the guys are his friends, he is wrong. "Do you think of the team as your friends, Drystan?"

"No."

"Ugh, that's what Ari said. You guys just don't see it, do you?"

"Aridam can be dense sometimes. Of course I see it. I just don't think of them as merely friends. They're my family. It's deeper than friendship; chosen family is everything to a high-level demon. If you think about it, most of our parents are low-level demons, meaning they aren't exactly good people. Terrible, even. We learned pretty quickly to depend on only each other." He looks at me, maintaining soft eye contact. "You're my family, too, now, Rhys. I'll always have your back."

"Oh, umm . . ." I look away as my eyes prickle. "That's, uh
. . ." I have to clear my throat; there seems to be a lump in
it. "I'd like that, I think. To be your family." Drystan
smirks and pats the table before standing and leaving me
with my own thoughts. These demons are hell on a man's
delicate sensibilities.

Aridam and Devland saunter in while I'm trying to get my
shit together. I give Dev a teary smile and a small wave
before I'm hauled over Ari's shoulder and marched from
the room.

"There are sandwiches in the fridge, Dev! Help yourself!"
I call before we are out of earshot.

In our room, Ari gently tosses me on the bed. He is quick
to cover me with his body, holding himself up by his
elbows so his weight doesn't crush me. He rubs his thumb
under my eye and across my cheek.

"Why were you crying, sweet Rhys? Tell me."

I give him a small chuckle. No doubt he felt emotion
through the bond that wasn't sadness and it left him
scrambling. "Just emotional, big guy."

"You should always be smiling, my mate. You didn't feel
upset so I was surprised seeing your tears, but I admit I
don't know what to do here."

"Kiss?" I just want his touch.

"That I will always give you." He leans down, nipping my bottom lip, coaxing my mouth open so he can plunder it. It's not an aggressive assault, more sensual and sweet. Our kisses stay lazy, no real rush to get off.

He slowly turns us so I'm on top of him, straddling his hips. He sits up just long enough to pull his shirt over his head. I take in his encouraging look and do the same. I gather some courage.

"Can I explore you? I want to know every inch of both your forms."

His breath catches, and with wide eyes, he gives me a small smile. I take that as permission and lean down, licking a path from his jaw to the hollow of his throat, eliciting a groan from him. My hands stroke over his broad shoulders, down his pecs, stopping to tease his piercing. He'd undressed fully at mock speed. I don't even remember him doing so, but I appreciate the view. His mouth falls slack and his breathing turns heavy, but I continue my wandering.

I scoot down his bare body, paying special attention to his deep V with my mouth, sucking marks into his skin. My hands dip around to the parts of his back and hips that are still accessible, the touch so light, it causes goosebumps I'm more than happy to soothe with my tongue.

I reach the apex of his thighs, marveling at the size and unique shape of him, but not touching, not yet. I grab the backs of his knees, and he allows me to spread him, baring himself to me fully. I run a thumb over his crease, circling his dark hole. His back curves up, offering me more. I can't take him up on the temptation or I'll never finish my exploration. I stroke down his legs to the bottom of his feet where his foot twitches like it tickles. I smirk, knowing I found a spot I doubt he's let anyone else near.

"Flip over, big guy."

With a grunt, he flips again, faster than I thought was warranted. I didn't even get to see his dick smack around. Pity. I do get a full view of his perfect ass and sculpted back, so it's still a win. I had started removing my pants, but I don't want to tear my eyes away for another second. I start from the bottom this time, tracing his muscles with my tongue. I pause to lavish attention on his gloriously firm ass, loving the way he arches up into my mouth.

The noises escaping him are so sexy. Grunts and groans, masculine and deep. Dipping my tongue into the dimples in his lower back, I let my hands roam everywhere, gripping and tracing his defined muscles. I reach his shoulder blades and suck marks into the space I know his wings sit in his other form. He moans louder, slightly humping the bed.

"No more, baby." Ari turns over, almost unseating me in the process. He pulls me up to him, devouring my mouth. He yanks the rest of my clothes off, rubbing his slick cock against mine. The ribbing feels so fucking good. I can feel Wrath just beneath the surface, pushing at him.

"Want you to come apart in my mouth, sweet Rhys. Need to taste you again."

"Ungh! Yes, please!"

I scramble to straddle his shoulders facing his cock, barely fitting our bodies together. Our size difference makes sixty-nine difficult. We've tried before, but it seems, like me, Ari doesn't care and wants to try again. I can get an inch of him in my mouth this way, his swollen head resting on my tongue. I suck softly. I groan as I get a shot of pre-come as it leaks out of him. I wait as patiently as possible for him to arrange the rest of my body how he sees fit. He finally pulls my erection between my legs and bunches in a crunch position, swallowing me down in one go. My moan (manly, manly squeal) is muffled around him, but it seems to spur him on more. He thrusts what he can into my mouth, gagging me slightly. Thank God he's so bendy and strong.

I reach down, bracing myself on his abdomen with one hand and rolling his balls in the other. They're so heavy. I gently pull them away from his body, and he gives a pleasured shout. His efforts double, the suction on my dick almost painful in its intensity. I pull my mouth off him to throw my head back. My moan is choppy, and I garble some kind of warning. The telltale tingle rushes through me, and I scream out my orgasm as he sucks it all down, never pausing his bobbing rhythm. Once my cock can't handle any more, I try to wriggle away. He lets me this time, though he doesn't always.

Ari's cock is a work of art in either form. Now that I can move, I scoot closer to it. The ribbing on his dick is a centimeter or so thick, spaced every inch down his length. I trace the ridges with my tongue, loving the texture of him. Using both hands to jerk him, I seal my mouth over what I can fit in there. It's still only about halfway because his girth is insane. He has shown me he likes gentle sucking but hard strokes. It only takes a second of suction before his mouth starts spewing praise and lewd phrases.

"Oh, that's it, baby, take it." His hands roam over my back and ass, squeezing my cheeks and pulling them apart, giving him a great view of my hole. "So pretty, baby. All puffy still from this morning. Is my seed still in there?" I grunt. I can't help the flexing of my inner muscles, knowing I'm still coated in him. His thumb settles against my hole, not moving. "I can feel you twitching, sweet

Rhys, so hot. Ungh! You're gonna make me come. You are going to swallow it all. I'm right there, baby, don't stop. Don't. Stop!" He floods my mouth, and I swallow convulsively, not wanting to miss a drop. With the sheer volume of it all, a tiny bit does trickle out of the corner of my mouth. When his cock softens, I let it go with an audible pop. He wastes no time pulling me back into his chest, using his thumb to push what little had escaped back onto my tongue.

"Good boy."

All I can do is hum my agreement. I never got to explore his demon form. Next time.

- - -

Kek has a reason to be so full of himself. I've never seen anyone move so smoothly. The grace he possesses with weapons in his hands is impressive but nothing compared to just his body. His teaching style is actually really nice. Better than how Lily would make me do the same motion over and over. Kek demands for me to follow the way my body naturally moves. Working on anticipating my opponents, reading aggressive body language.

It was fine training in the alley behind the store when it was just me and Lily, but the chance of someone stumbling across us is higher during the day. The den we took over is smaller, making it harder to re-enact an actual fight, but that doesn't seem to bother the demons taking turns training me.

"You're small. You have to be fast, be smart. A staff will do nothing to most supernaturals. They'll overpower you before you get a second swing in." He looks so haughty, but I can read him better after our afternoon together. He's just being honest with me.

"Running will get you killed. Tripping a predator's prey drive is the last thing you want."

He goes into detail on what to do with each race. Playing dead won't deter a vampire; they'll feel your heartbeat and drain you anyway. A shifter enjoys playing with their food, so the more you resist, the worse it'll get. Stalling until a team member can get to me is the goal.
 "I know the idea of being bitten by anyone other than your mate hurts, but you have to prepare. At least you'll be alive."

After another hour of working my ass off, he calls it a day.

"Aridam has to be chomping at the bit to whisk you away. Let him. It's hard for a demon to feel their mate struggle."

"I have to cover Devland at the shop downstairs." Kek's snort accompanies my statement, telling me how likely actually heading downstairs is.

I'm surprised when we exit the temporary training room and don't see Ari there waiting for me. Where is my demon? I check our bond and find him to be fine, if not a little curious.

Following the short hall to the kitchen, I come up empty. Kek checks his phone and swears.

"Meeting room, they found something."
We rush down, noting the shop has already been cleared out and closed. Once inside the meeting room, we split up. Kek finds his seat next to Kieran, while I look for the empty seat next to Ari I thought he'd save for me. Instead, he scoots his chair back and I climb on up, the group not even pausing in their conversation while I settle myself. I feel Wrath's purring rumble through my back, and I squeeze his arm that had wrapped around me in greeting.

I don't want to interrupt, so I listen carefully as they detail the documents they found at a summer estate in Colorado. The coven house there had been deserted, seemingly left in a hurry. They pass around photos showing overturned furniture and food rotten at tables. It's as if an entire group of people had simply disappeared.

"There didn't seem to be anything big taken. None of the normal signs of packing, just the chaos of a large group fleeing in a panic." Drystan seems resigned.

"The scent of blood was strong, but no physical evidence of a struggle was present. No broken doors or obvious damage. It's just messy," Azvameth chimes in.

"We couldn't scent anything other than vampire, but there was one that seemed off. I did also pick up whiffs of a familiar smell, either Constantine or someone close to him. The scent was there the night Aridam and I were attacked." Drystan then points to a few of the pictures still lying on the table. "These show medical journals someone has been meticulously keeping on various elevations in hormones in different species of shifters. It doesn't seem to be a complete work, more like pages left behind."

"On accident or on purpose?" I'm startled by my own question.

"What do you mean, mate?" Ari asks.

"Well, the only place that seems to be organized still is the medical rooms. So why leave seemingly important pages behind? They were found like they'd been dropped but not crumpled, like they were in a binder and others in a notebook. They weren't throwaways; they look to have been taken out of the binding, not torn."

"Very good, Rhys. I was thinking that myself. Who would want someone interfering with Constantine's work, though, if they were helping him?" Kek's question isn't rhetorical but feels like it.

Everyone remains silent, not having an answer.

"We have more addresses to investigate, but I don't think we should wait to move on the estate. The likelihood of the souls being stashed at the smallest of the safe houses is slim," Devland throws in.

"I agree. There's next to no security at the rest, and while he's a major douchebag, Constantine isn't stupid. I haven't been able to hack the estate's system yet, but my programs should be done within twenty-four hours." I love seeing Belial so close to the team. No more hiding in the hall.

"What are the chances that you all can get in and out without causing a commotion? Would it be better to try for stealth instead of distraction?" I must be on a roll, asking these questions. I catch an impressed look from a few of the guys, and the bond hums with pride.

"Distraction is really our only option. They'll be able to feel us enter their wards. We need to split up again." Drystan's comment sends the team into another round of discussion. I lean back, resting my head on Ari's chest. Training today kicked my ass. I want to just relax in my mate's arms for a while. I let my mind drift, soaking up Ari's warmth and letting Wrath's purr lull me into a half-asleep but semi-aware state. Funny, meditation normally makes me want to rip my hair out.

Az claps his hands, refocusing everyone and startling me into being fully awake. "So we scout ahead, Belial does his tech magic, and we hit two places at once as a distraction. It leaves the third team to slip in and grab the souls. We have no idea what condition we will find them in. Team one is myself and Drystan; team two is Kieran and Aridam.

"Bel, we'll need you to be watching for all of us. The accuracy depends completely on the comms. It's the leg up we need. After Devland and Kek secure the souls, we all portal to Reception together. I know it's a lot to leave to chance, but this is all we've got."

Mumbles of approval follow his layout of their plan.

Chapter Ten

Rhys

I wish I could do more. It's not like I'm a good fighter; I have very little value until it comes time to help the people being held by Constantine. I can snark with the best of them. Scrappy like a normal foster kid but nothing crazy. Strong enough to haul kegs at work but not compared to the demons around the table. The only reason I can even sit here is because I'm Ari's mate. I am a Null, though; I can dampen the effects of all magic, like with Belial's leak. Maybe "sneaky smother fucker" is a skill they'll appreciate (pun definitely intended).

I didn't realize I had been mumbling most of this out loud, or that the table had gotten quiet, until Kieran reaches over and taps my hand. I jerk my head up, almost knocking into Ari's chin, and the lust demon winks at me.

"Oh, that's embarrassing," Kek stage whispers at the same time Ari gives a firm, "No." That definitely gets my attention.

"What do you mean no? I want to help!" The tension rises in the room; it's almost palpable. "I'm not just going to sit here and listen to everyone else have a job for the plan that requires you to walk into danger AGAIN. I can't handle you coming back injured like that again, Ari. What use is being a Null if I can't help?"

Bel's soft voice comes from beside me, soothing. "I need help with the tech side, Rhys. Another set of eyes would go a long way."

"Lily could watch with you. She'd come back for that. I can help out there, I promise." I'm talking to more than just Bel. I maintain eye contact as best I can with Ari while sitting on his knee, his eyes flashing.

"I need you safe, mate. I won't be able to focus if you're there."

I deflate, knowing I'd hate to risk his focus, but I can do better out there than here. Bracing for his anger, I keep pushing. "I'll walk ahead of you and disable any magical traps. I won't be in any danger. You'll be right there, and it'll give you even more time to get into position. Someone can pop me back here before the fighting starts, or I can go with Kek and help with the souls."

Devland pipes up in my defense. "It's not a bad plan, Aridam. You know Kek and I can protect him, and the souls will be more cooperative if there's a non-demon there. He'll be fine, I promise."

I can feel how torn he is. I give him the best "badass" scowl I can muster. My chest twinges, but he finally

117

relents. I want to say it's the scowl, but I probably looked like an angry kitten compared to . . . well, everyone else.

"You'll guard him with your life, Devland. If one hair is misplaced, I won't be able to hold Wrath back." Eyes wide, everyone at the table nods. "We leave in six hours. Be ready."

With that, he stands, yanking me up from his lap and throwing me over his shoulder. I let out one of my super manly squeals as he slaps my ass. Upside down, I wave to the guys before I'm out of sight. Ari switches to a bridal hold as he marches to our room and then throws me on the bed. I have time to do absolutely nothing before his body covers mine, my wrists grasped in one of his hands and stretched above my head.

"Naughty mate. Do you know what I would do if something happened to you? I'd burn the world down."

Honestly that shouldn't have made my dick twitch . . . but alas, if it could twerk, that's what it'd be doing. "Good thing we won't have to find out. Now kiss me? I've been hard since I walked into the meeting!" I am whining by the end, the pressure on my wrists increasing.

His kiss steals my breath, and I can't stay still. My body has a mind of its own, arching my chest to meet his, using my bound wrists as leverage. My ass is still a little sore from last night, but I don't care. I need the burn right now. I'm drowning in our combined arousal, my need to feel him own me overwhelming everything else.

"This won't be gentle, sweet Rhys," he warns. He's said that before and everything was perfect.

"Use me, big guy. I want the real you." I can't forget the crazy stretch his demon form had forced on my body during our mating. I need it again, to have him know I'll take all of him.

I continue to undulate, practically humping his muscular torso. His body grows against me, pressing down. Wings snap out, splayed behind him. His free hand cuts my shirt down the middle with a single claw. He doesn't stop in the downward path, snagging my pants and pale-blue briefs and cutting them from my body too. The hand holding me in place doesn't falter, maintaining that trapped feeling I crave from my demon. It only increases as I feel his tail wrap around my calf, pulling my legs wider. He had leaned back a little to watch the unwrapping, but now that we're both properly naked, his mouth takes mine again. I'm panting, not able to really kiss back. I lick his bottom lip, and as he opens, I slide my tongue along one of his long fangs. His shudder sends a thrill through me. It still blows my mind that I can affect someone so powerful. I do it again and he growls, flipping me over and pulling me onto my knees. The hand holding my wrists loosens and slides down to rest between my shoulders, pressing me into the bed.

"Fuck, baby, look at you." He rubs my left cheek and pulls it lightly to the side, exposing me fully. His grip changes but doesn't loosen as he lowers himself onto the bed behind me. My breathing picks up in anticipation. He's just staring. I start to feel overly exposed, unsure, but it's wiped away into nothing at the first swipe of his forked tongue. I cry out, unable to hold it in. His tongue should be illegal. He eats me like he's starving, his tongue wriggling its way into my body, flicking back and forth. I've never felt anything like it, obviously. My orgasm barrels through me. I've never come untouched, though I've come close with toys. This feels a million times stronger. I hump back onto his face, riding it out to his approving moans.

He finally pulls out, immediately shoving a thick digit in, then three. That's all the prep we can handle before I'm being split apart in the best way. I'm shocked when my dick slaps against my stomach, hard again already.

"I'm going to wreck this ass, sweet Rhys. God, you were made for me. Just mine, only mine. Hold on, baby." He had given me enough time to adjust, but barely. His thrusts start off punishing, no slow buildup, and I revel in this small loss of control. I feel like his cock is rearranging my insides, I'm so full. I can't speak, can barely moan. I feel myself close to drooling, my mind blank, concentrating on feeling everything my mate is doing to me. His hips slap my ass; he lifts me to meet his thrusts, my lower half completely off the bed. Only my hands touch the mattress.

Reaching down, he uses one arm to pull my back to his chest. Using me like I begged him to. I feel like a sex doll being manhandled. Newest kink un-fucking-locked. My hands reach up to secure myself to the arm holding me against him.

The tail I haven't truly become acquainted with snakes around up my throat, squeezing just enough before sliding between my parted lips. I suck instinctively around the heart-shaped barb. His thrusts become faster, choppier. I feel him swelling and know he'll come soon. He won't come until I do, though. I can feel his need to mark me again in my chest.

Just knowing he'll fill me up again, paired with the hammering of my prostate, sets me off. I scream, the muffled sound so dirty around the tail still fucking my mouth. My vision blurs around the edges, and I feel myself going limp. His heat spreads through me, and I let go, giving in to the floaty darkness.

Aridam

If we hadn't bonded, I would be losing my shit right now. I know he's just passed out from the intensity of his multiple orgasms, but having him go limp so suddenly scared me. I can feel his satisfaction echoing through me even as I slip from his body. Wrath preens like a peacock at having fucked his mate unconscious without even touching his pretty little dick. I don't want to leave Rhys dirty, so with my tail, I grab a rag from the pile I put next to the bed. I don't want to put my sweet mate down yet, so I hold him while I clean him up.

We don't have much time before we need to head out, but I want to let him rest. I'd rather he stay here with Bel, safe in a tower, as they say, but Rhys is incredibly stubborn. I knew if I didn't agree, he would find a way to sneak into Constantine's, anyway. At least I can protect him better if he isn't trying to hide from me.

He snuggles into my chest, and I gently lower him onto the side of the bed that's not covered in come. I grin wryly, not being able to hold back the flush of pride. So perfect, watching him come completely undone.

I turn to head toward the shower, pulling my demon form back in. It's much easier to shower when I can actually fit into it. I don't dally, just a quick in and out, and rejoin my mate. His soft snores are endearing. I lean down over the bed and kiss his forehead.

"Sweet Rhys, we have to get ready."

"Fuck off." It's mumbled, but I hear it nonetheless.

I can't help but chuckle. So prickly for being so sated. I stroke my hand up his shoulder and grip his neck, squeezing.
"Naughty Rhys. Get up."

He shivers at the tone in my voice, peeking over the covers. His scowl isn't the least bit intimidating, and he must feel my humor, because it intensifies.

"Fine! I need another coffee, anyway."

I smooth the wrinkle between his brows with my thumb. His skin is so soft everywhere, and he gives me a shy smile. I pick him up, cradling him to me. My intention was to set him down so he could dress, but he seems to have a different idea.

Thirty minutes and another shower later, we're ready to head out. I check in with the team, shooting quick texts as I wait for Rhys to make his coffee. I note how he doctors it with an elephant's share of cream and sugar. He must feel my revulsion through the bond, because he sasses me with his eyebrows. I didn't know one could do so much talking while simultaneously drinking.

"Lemme guess, you're a black-coffee drinker?" He says it with a shudder, like I had just told him I eat shit for breakfast.

"No, just a normal amount of sweetener. That's not even coffee anymore, mate."

"Shut your beautiful mouth hole. It's the best I can do with the sludge Lily has here."

I wrinkle my nose doubtfully. He goes on, changing the subject to avoid more judgement, leaning against the kitchen island.

"Oh! I do have questions, if you have some time?"

"I'll do my best to answer." I brace myself, putting my phone in my pocket. I have no idea what will come out of his mouth. A deep inhale is followed by a stream of consciousness I have trouble keeping up with.

"I never got an answer about the freaky frozen neighbors, and I'm dying to know how they turned all human popsicle on me. Does it hurt to go through a portal? Will it work on me since I'm a Null? I didn't want to bring it up before in case I got shut down. Is your tail super sensitive like your horns? Can you control it like another arm? Do your wings come out in demon form all the time or just when you want to? Does the whole team look the same in their forms? I saw Drystan, and he looked a little different, being grey instead of red, but otherwise, he's built like you are. Are all demons as attractive as your team?

"Not that I want to fuck them, I'm not that kind of guy. I've been cheated on; I wouldn't wish that on anyone. You said I was yours when we mated and that you wouldn't let me go. Does that go both ways? I think I'd die if you got a different mate. Lily said normally you only get one soulmate, but you got a second chance, so what if you decide to try for a third?

"Gah, that didn't come out right. You know what I mean. It might be too early to throw around the big L, but you know how I feel, right? You have to. I can feel you, too, most of the time, but it's hard to understand which feelings are whose. If either of us is injured, will we feel their pain or just that they *are* in pain?

"Is there a way for me to fix Bel? He's so lonely, it makes me wanna cry. I don't want to be the weak link on the job later—is there anything I should know about the guys' routines before we leave? Do you use hand signals like in movies, or just the comms?" He trails off at the end, finally registering the horror on my face. So. Many. Questions.

I am stuck on one thing he said. I need to touch him while we talk about this, so I round the island and pick him up under his armpits, careful of his coffee, and set him on the counter. Our faces are closer, but not by much, so I lean down until we're eye to eye.

"I need to address one thing before I try to sift through all of that. You are mine and I am yours. I won't even see another being as more than a friend for the rest of our lives. I *really* don't like thinking of you with past lovers, but any guy has to be an imbecile to stray from you. You're everything I could have dreamed of. This isn't like what humans do while fishing. I'm not just going to throw you back if you aren't big enough. You are my perfect other half."

"You really feel that way?" His chin wobbles.

"With everything I am," I promise. He tucks himself against me.

"What about the rest?"

"The rest?" I parrot back. I'm so confused.

"I asked you a bajillion questions and the only thing that stuck was a mate question?"

"Well, yeah, it was important." I wrack my brain. "Umm . . . maybe start writing them down? I, uh . . . don't remember what you asked."

"Hmm . . . I can do that. How efficient. Maybe I can text questions to Bel, too, as I think of them. I don't want to bombard any one person, though you definitely already knew this about me before you signed on the dotted line."

I snort. "I did. I'm sure everyone would be happy to answer some, but I like that you come to me." I kiss the top of his head, loving how soft his hair is against my lips.

"Me too. My God, your pecs are so firm. When did you get this?" He pinches my nipple, the one with a small bar through it.

"Not too long ago, actually. I lost a bet with Devland. I forget it's there most of the time."

He pinches both nipples this time, making my cock jerk. "Which one is more sensitive? Does it feel really good?"

"Fuck. Yeah, it does, but you had questions." I hate myself for reminding him. He doesn't stop playing with them, but his attention was diverted to getting answers once again.

"Oh, right! A few really do need to be answered now. Like portals. Can I even use them?"

"They *are* magic; I'm actually not sure. I should call Astaroth and give an update, anyway. We can ask him." I pull my phone back out and dial our duke. I pull Rhys's hands away from my abused nipples, and he flushes.

"Ahh, Aridam. I was wondering when I would be getting a call. The men have been keeping me updated, so I'm assuming the call is about the Null you seem to have acquired."

"Yes, sir, about that. Rhys, he's actually . . . he's my mate."

"Congratulations, Aridam. After this clusterfuck is over, you will receive your mating vacation package and get your paperwork updated in Hell, correct?" I hear him talk to someone, I'm guessing his assistant.

"Yes, sir. We did have a few questions, though, about how this will work while on assignment. We were going to portal him, but will he be able to use one? I've never actually interacted with a Null before, and Rhys is new to this."

"I see. Your mating bond will bend this a little. Your portals should work because they are a part of you."

I hate asking, "And what about the twin soul bond?"

"Interesting. Who has your little mate bonded to?"

"Belial." I try not to growl it.

"Oh my, that's quite a pairing. I look forward to watching this play out. Anyway, the bond might not be strong enough to matter. You could always test it. The worst that could happen is that nothing happens at all. Do let me know, though. I need to check on a few things, but I have some leads on how living arrangements will work for you and your mate. We can't have him expire if you portal him home to meet me."

I wince. I didn't think about that. As a duke, Astaroth cannot leave Hell for more than a few hours at a time, a day at most.

"Yes, sir."

"Good. Keep me informed, Aridam. It seems your team's reports aren't as thorough as I thought they'd be."

"Yes, sir."

Rhys snorts wildly. I can tell he's trying to hold himself together. Thankfully Astaroth hangs up so Rhys can howl and slap his leg. He's completely overcome with laughter.

"Yes, sir, yes, sir, yes, sir! Oh God, that was funny. You know he sounded like he was teasing you, right?"

Did he? I'm not so sure. Astaroth is not really a teasing kind of guy. I switch the subject, and like the sweet man he is, he lets me with minimal smirking.

Chapter Eleven

Rhys

We've tested portal after portal, and the only one I can go through is Ari's. This kinks our plan just a tad. Wrath will have to come find me and help Devland and Kek portal the souls over, since I'd be stuck there otherwise. I can tell it makes him incredibly worried, but it's not a huge deal from where I'm sitting.

"You were going to portal me around, anyway. I don't understand why it's making you freak like this."

"Yes, Rhys, because I wanted to, not because I was the only option! What I want is for you to be able to get to safety without worrying about your proximity to me!"

"Can we do this in your room? I know they can still hear us." I look to the closed door to the pantry. It's the only thing between us and his team.

"Our room. We'll just talk again later. I know I'm being unreasonable, but even Wrath is freaking out."

I slump down. "I get it, but this is still the best plan. I trust you to get me out of there when we need to. Trust your team; they'll make sure I'm okay until you can take over, okay?"

"Fine. I won't bring it up again. I'm still not happy about it, though."

I get a scorching kiss, and then he's back in the conference room, all business.

It takes an hour to secure our gear. I get a fancy bulletproof vest and tactical gear to match the team. Comms are fit and have been checked a million times. Bel doesn't seem nervous, which actually helps my anxiety. I take Ari's hand and double-check my vest pocket for the pouch of crystals Lily gave me. They're the only things stopping vamps from immediately sensing our blood. My humanness is a little harder to conceal, but we did the best we could. The room shimmers ahead of me, and the pairs start walking through. Kieran jumps through his own portal right before I step through Ari's. I feel like I'm going to throw up, but yakking all over my mate's boots will not inspire trust that I can handle this. Too bad he can feel my nausea through the bond. He rubs small circles on my back, soothing me while I get my shit together.

Once I no longer fear my lunch coming back up, I step forward. Drystan had drawn me a map, so I know which path to take to disable any traps. I keep myself a few yards ahead of the group, picking the easiest route.

Through the whole perimeter, we only find one trap for me to stand on while they pass me. I have to hold each of their hands to make the magic glide over us. Going in sets of three doesn't take too long. Ari kisses me deeply before calling on his demon form. Through the bond, I feel Wrath ready to fuck shit up. I can see the moment Ari steps back. Wrath is front and center, and he looks like a murderous kid in a candy store. Giddy, almost bouncing. I keep my giggle inside but wink at him. He kisses my forehead, grabs Kieran, and takes off toward the front.

Drystan sprints to the side, followed by Az at a glacial pace. Kek rolls his eyes but then tilts his chin toward the back, where he, Devland, and I will sneak in.

I hear Wrath roar and a loud crash. Yelling comes from inside the mansion (coven estate my ass; this place looks like a Kardashian could live here if they had no taste). I'm not worried about Wrath; his excitement hasn't waned, though the sound of the sheer number of vampires pouring out of the house is insane.

I hear the clicking of keys on Bel's computer in my ear; he hasn't said a word since the check-in after the trap at the border. "Team three, go." Fuck, okay, our turn.

I grab the back door, feeling magic slide up my arm. I just continue to hold it, like waiting for a sand timer to finish. I just want to scream *hurry up!* but it's like waiting for water to boil. Finally, the magic seems to dissipate, so I step back. Devland steps up and twists the locked knob, breaking it off. With a gentle push, the door glides open without creaking. We shuffle inside, passing the kitchen. We had agreed not to split up onto different floors, but Kek starts heading down the hall to the right, away from where Devland and I are. I raise a brow at Dev, getting an eye roll back. He grabs my wrist and tugs me along to check the rooms to the left.

Belial must have finally hacked into all the cameras, because he chimes in, "Basement has cells. Some are empty, but there's something down there you guys need to check out. I can't see past a certain point, but my gut says we need to take a look. Main level is clear, and second floor has three rooms without cameras . . . and you guys are running out of time."

"Shit. Okay, Rhys and I will take the basement. Bel, let Kek know to take upstairs." Devland urges me back the way we came.

"He'll be fine. We have to go," he tries to reassure me. I don't like the idea of Kek going alone where we can't get to him, but I don't really have a choice. We walk back toward the stairs we passed by the kitchen. Another spell. I grab Dev's hand and walk through it, hoping that will be enough like it was outside. The magic seems to be passive, not aggressive. Huh. It's weird, knowing something like that without knowing why. The stairs creak, and the finished basement with a pool table and a bar is not what I expected to find. Where would they hide a cell? Bel answers my unspoken question.

"At the end of the hall to the left is a door disguised as a bookshelf. Was probably built as a panic room. Check for a button or switch." We race to the ornate bookcase I would have sworn was a built-in. Devland sweeps the shelves clean, revealing a pull latch behind a weird-as-fuck statue. I reach out to pull it and am hit with another spell. It washes around me angry as fuck, lashing around my skin almost like fire. I shiver; I'd be super dead if I were a normal human.

"Hurry, Rhys. I can hear the guys out front. Kieran is injured and Az is running out of steam. Kek cleared the rooms upstairs; he's headed your way," Belial says into my ear.

"I'm trying! It's super fucking angry, Bel. If I don't wait long enough, it'll blow up me and everything else in the room—including whatever is behind here."

"Take your time, Rhys. If we need more time, Aridam and Drystan can keep them occupied." Devland is trying to sound composed, but the urgency isn't completely wiped from his voice.

Well, fuck. I don't want Wrath fighting longer than he has to. Right on cue, we hear a monstrous roar paired with the dual-toned screech I imagine a dinosaur would make.

A slow smile covers Devland's face, his eyes lighting up with excitement.

"Drystan let his control on his need for gluttony slip." He comes close to clapping his hands like a little demon cheerleader.

The magic calms down enough for me to push the door open. It reveals a decently large concrete room with cells on the right and chains hanging on the left from giant hooks in the ceiling. A medical table catches my attention at the back of the room, complete with machines and a desk with papers overwhelming the corner space. Troughs covered in dried blood litter the floor. Fuck, this is horrific. They're torturing and bleeding people out like some modern-day Báthory fantasy. Revulsion makes saliva pool in my mouth, stomach cramping, and I know I have to step out or I'll throw up everywhere.

I gag and point to the hall we just came through, and Devland nods solemnly. I see Kek walking toward us, and he steps past me on my way out, patting my shoulder. I keep going, only leaning against the wall once I'm far enough away that I can't smell blood and death. In front of me is another bookcase . . .

"Bel?"

"Yeah?"

"There's another bookcase. Is it also some sick torture room?"

"There's no camera. I don't know. I can't even see you right now. Go back to where I can get eyes on you, Rhys."

"I'm going to check." From what I saw, the souls aren't in there, but I know Kek and Dev will be thorough.

"Wait for one of the guys, Rhys!"

"There's no time." I sweep the shelf, thinking if there's a latch, it will be the same kind as last time. I grin when I see it, grabbing and waiting. Not as aggressive, but still strong. I hear a noise behind me, but there's nothing there. I need to hurry. The door pushes open without me pulling it, and I find six people huddled in the corner of a small concrete room. It smells like pure filth, making my eyes water. I take a step in and sweep the room, spotting someone with white-blond hair lying almost lifeless on the floor. My heart clenches and I rush over to him, calling for Bel, Kek, anyone.

A crackling from the comm is my only response. I would normally stop to think shit through a little more, but this is Taylor. He doesn't look right. His delicate fingers are blue-grey at the tips, and bruises and bloody dots cover his whole body. I can fit my hand in the divot above his collarbones. He looks like a skeleton with skin.

I feel for a pulse; it's thready but there, I think. I've never had to check a maybe-dead body before. Movement from the huddle of people in the corner catches my eye. One of the men has moved forward into a protective stance, while the others look terrified. Someone whimpers. I spin to look at the door, expecting to see Kek or Devland, but again, no one is there. The fuck? A breeze behind me is the only warning I have before everything goes black.

- - -

Awareness comes in slowly, my brain fuzzy and disjointed. Fuck, my whole body hurts. My arms scream from being stretched over my head, shoulders already fucked up. I'm hanging from what I assume is a similar contraption to the things in the torture room at the mansion. I take stock of the rest of my body before I open my eyes. I'm pretty sure I'm naked; the weight of my vest is gone, and the cool air brushes against my clammy skin.

Trying to keep my breathing steady is difficult. My ribs and head throb. Nothing feels broken. I send out a quick thanks to the powers that be. I remember being knocked out, but nothing after, so I have no idea how long I've been unconscious. My bond is going wild, fury and worry so strong it hurts. I crack my eyes just a sliver, trying to gauge if I'm alone. Nope, no such luck.

"Ah, he's awake. So happy you could join us," Creep Number One says in a jovial tone. I don't respond, watching the two men warily.

"Come now, you must know who I am?" This must be Constantine. I nod, wincing at the sharp pain it causes.

"Perfect! Then you know why you're here." Not really, but I won't be asking them to elaborate quite yet. Creep Number Two hasn't said a word, just staring at me with dead eyes. He's built like a brick shithouse. I've always disliked the phrase, but it's fitting. He looks like a pale bodybuilder with a dash of Russian mobster. It's the shaved head, I think, that gives the Russian feel. The dark-red rings around his eyes lend a haunted look. Constantine catches my gaze and starts an introduction of sorts.
 "This is Ivan. Not an original name, but he doesn't care what I call him, do you, Ivan?"

Not even a muscle twitch from the lackey. Haha! I was right, Russian. Well, at least some Russian heritage.

"He's my most effective blood-letter. I knew when the demons came, I needed to bring him along with my experiments. Too bad you're the only one we could grab before we had to skedaddle . . ." He continues droning on, but my focus shifts.

My feet feel wet, not just clammy. I look down and will my eyes to focus. Once they do, I regret looking. I'm bleeding from seemingly random cuts that range in size on my legs and feet. I can't help but stare at the tiny red rivers, absorbed in watching them connect and separate like a spider web down to my toes before dripping off. They don't really hurt, just feel warm. Huh.

Constantine snaps his fingers. "Pay attention, human. Did you know that you should have died already? Ivan thinks you're a bonded Null, but we have to make sure. The bonded part we know—your mark is pretty recent—but the rest? It would be a wonderful boon, you know, to have a human who won't die after a rigorous feeding and will hamper any tracking spells. Imagine what we could do. A pity about your body, though. So fragile, even after bonding. I haven't tasted you yet; I wonder if you'll give the same boost a shifter does. Ivan here gets first taste in case he's wrong and your blood kills us instead. Such fun!"

He's deranged. "You're a card or two short of a full deck, cocoa puffs. You know they'll find me, right?" I mean, I hope so. I won't be the person who hopes the love of their life just leaves them behind to save themselves . . . ew. I want my badass demon to come rip this crazy man apart. I know he'll come. Hopefully Wrath lets Ari take over soon, though. It feels like he's on a mindless rampage, and I can't think it's a productive one. My vision fades a little, and I know I'm going to pass out eventually.

"We're counting on it, human. Demon blood is an acquired taste. So smoky . . . rare. Not many vampires are willing to attack a demon to get some, but it's so worth it. I've only gotten greed demon before, low level. I wonder how a high-level wrath demon will feel." He shivers in pleasure at the thought. I don't know if he's aware Wrath is my mate or if he's just naming the sin he wants a bite of next.

My stomach churns. I don't know how long I can do this without my brain breaking, but I'll hold out as long as possible. Passing out is a sweet oblivion, giving me the rest I know I'll need.

Chapter Twelve

Aridam

The pain echoing through my bond with Rhys is enough of a distraction to finally wrestle control from Wrath. The red haze faded hours ago, but his rampage didn't end with it. Our mate is missing and we can't feel him. Everything else is secondary.

I look around the decimated estate, spying a few tells that at least part of my team is still here in the shadows. I pick my way across what's left of the courtyard, stepping on a stray body part here and there. I find Drystan propped against a nearby stump, cradling his arm. Wrath had snapped it when Drys had tried to pull him away from the vampires that were already very, very dead. He had shouted about it not helping anything to rip them apart, that we needed answers. After my . . . outburst . . . he slinked quietly away.

I smoothly pull in my demon form and approach my best friend with a decent amount of trepidation. He arches one brow once I'm close enough to really see his face.

"I'm sorry, Drys. I couldn't control him."
"Under the current circumstances, it's understandable. I forgive you. You're lucky my sin is so satisfied that I feel

like humans do after Thanksgiving dinner. Pull that shit again and I'll kick your ass." I know he's not kidding. We aren't an even match—Wrath would rip him apart—but the ferocity needed to do so wouldn't be present. I feel a begrudging acceptance from Wrath that he deserves an ass kicking. Too bad I'd face the consequences right along with him.

"Want to head to the shop? See what Bel has come up with?" he asks as he holds his good hand out for me to help him up.

"Yeah, I lost my comm at some point. I don't know what happened past them finding a handful of the missing souls and Rhys gone." I feel like I'm going to puke. My *mate* is missing. My sweet mate.

"At least we know exactly when your little mate went missing. Your meltdown happened immediately after, so we know about how far they could have gotten by now. Let's go back." As he stands there, his arm hangs at an odd angle by his side. He must notice the direction of my stare. "I'll have Kek reset it at the shop . . . It's not healing as fast as it should. A lot of their weapons were obsidian."

"Yeah, okay." I feel a little lost. Helpless. I know Rhys is awake and in pain—I felt a surge of fear earlier, so I know he's not okay. I'm fighting Wrath now with every step. We portal back to Lily's, and I see everyone except Devland and Kek have gathered. Az dozes at the table, and it immediately pisses me off. I smack the table next to his head, startling him awake.

"Fuck, Aridam, what was that for?!"

"How can you be sleeping when *my mate is missing*?!" I'm roaring by the end, and I feel my skin twitching.

"He was out trying to connect with all your team's contacts to get more info about your mate, Aridam, while you were back at the mansion throwing a tantrum."

I flinch at the sound of Astaroth's voice. He looks decidedly unimpressed by my outburst. I sit at the table, making sure to keep my eyes averted, properly chastised. I didn't hear him, which is a huge misstep. I should be aware of everything around me at all times. My emotions make it impossible to focus. Wrath's demand for our mate is a constant thrum through my veins.

"Now, I need an update on your plan to retrieve Rhys before I head to see the souls." Astaroth glides to the head of the table, placing his hands on it, and leans forward, looking directly at me.

Bel pipes up to save my ass, his voice carrying from right outside the room. "We have video feed from the street cameras closest to the coven's estate. There was no activity there during our raid. The only thing I could find was a lone black SUV that sat a few miles down the road.

A blur appears to enter the vehicle two minutes after Aridam went nuclear, and another, bigger blur follows shortly after. From the pictures I could get off the feed, it looks like Constantine and two others. The third person could be Rhys based on body size and the fact that he was being carried. The SUV peels off, away from the city, heading southwest toward Jersey. We lose visual on them about ten minutes later; they seem to just disappear. I'm pulling the properties in connection to Constantine in that area, but it might take a bit."

I stay silent, suppressing the growl trying to tear out of my throat. He could be anywhere. New Jersey is only a three-hour drive from Great Neck. From there, they could have flown, driven, gotten on a fucking boat.

"Excellent work, Belial. Keep me posted on the search. I must go sort things out with Devland and Kek; they're having some problems with a few of the souls." He disappears; his portals don't really shimmer like ours.

Kieran is tentative, but I hear the need in his voice. "We need a few hours of rest before we go hunting Constantine. We're exhausted. We won't be good to anyone if we can't function. Bel, you can use bots for most of this, right? You need sleep, too, honey."

"No. I mean, yes, I can. But just for an hour. Then I can sort through the rest of the info here. Hopefully Devland will be back by then. He can help me," Belial concedes.

The rest of the team gets up and heads to crash, but I can't move. Staring at the cherry-colored tabletop, I can't imagine sleeping when something could happen to Rhys at any time. His pain has been constant since he woke up. It's not life-threatening yet, but I hate the thought of him enduring even a paper cut.

Drystan claps my shoulder as he passes, urging me to grab some sleep while I can. I nod, knowing I won't. I replay the whole night, including before we left. My mate was so brave, so beautiful in his defiance. I need him back, and now. Lost in thought, I don't notice Lily until she sets a mug in front of me.

"It's tea, demon. You need rest. This will help." I know she doesn't necessarily like me, not even after Liam fucked off and screwed her over. She cares about Rhys, though; everyone who meets him does. His incessant questions and huge heart, that perfectly placed snark that gets me all riled up.

"Thank you. I'll drink it." Maybe. She's not wrong; I need to recharge after tonight.

"I'll stay until it's gone." She looks at me expectantly.

"Fine, witch." I slam it back in a large gulp like a human at a shot bar, grimacing at the awful taste. "Done. Now go get some sleep yourself."

She gives a small nod. "We'll find him. He's strong; he'll make it through this. In the morning, I'll scry for Constantine again. I have someone grabbing me something of his in the rubble you left behind. Maybe we'll get lucky."

"One can hope." My eyes grow increasingly heavy. Drugged. Should have known. I don't make it back to the room, falling asleep right where I sit. The pull on my chest has gone quiet again, like he's falling asleep too . . . I can only hope it's something as innocent as sleep.

Rhys

I jerk awake this time. No gentle ascent to reality. The pain in my arms and down my back is excruciating. I can't hold back my sob, struggling to do something, anything.

"Hold still, human, you're ruining the experience." Fuck, I should have checked if I was alone, though I don't really give a shit. I'm feeling delirious at best. I feel a sharp pain on my back, behind my ribs. I grunt, trying to pull away from the feeling. I see Ivan in front of me, so the voice and accompanying pain must be coming from the resident quack-fuck. A vaguely familiar sound invades my ears. Is he moaning?! Fuck, I wanna vomit; I just don't have the energy.

146

"You didn't do him justice, Ivan. He's absolutely delicious. So pure." He steps into my vision, and I can see the blood dripping from his lip. Like he did it on purpose. How silly.

"You don't have to waste it, you know. It doesn't actually make you look intimidating. How crude, talking with food on your face." My voice is thready, but the snark is unmistakable. Nifty. If I'm going to be a temporary blood bag, I don't want to be particularly docile.

His eyes flash, and I see the predator lurking. Too bad he's not the scariest thing I've seen this week.

"Did I hurt your feelings? How sad for you. I would assume someone so ridiculously old would have thicker skin." Okay, well, there's a difference between snarky and just asking for him to kill me. Unfortunately, I'm not really in control of my mouth, so I keep going. "You look like a toddler playing dress-up as a monster. It must suck being stuck with . . . *that* for eternity. How relieved you must feel having a scary-looking vampire at your beck and call. Otherwise, no one would fear you, backstreet." I'm lying. He's incredibly attractive. His suit is perfect and the malice he exudes is frightening, but I'm sensing some short guy syndrome and can't help but to poke at it.

"Ahh, I see. To think I had a passing regret at not being able to make this painless for you. Compulsion is such an effective pain reliever." His snarl says he's losing it a little, that I'm affecting him. I need him just angry enough to knock me out, not kill me.

"Eh, I'll live." I'm funny. He doesn't seem to appreciate my humor, but I see a flash of amusement cross Ivan's face.

"Only because I say so, human. I could kill you right now."
"You could, but that wouldn't be very smart of you. Although not super scary, you don't strike me as stupid. Who am I to judge, though? You do you, boo-boo."

My refusal to call him by his name is intentional, and he finally looks properly disgusted. Who knew that would be the one to trip him up. I let out a whispery giggle. Wow, this blood-loss thing is trippy. Unfortunately, he chooses that moment to strike again, clamping his jaws right above my hip. My giggle turns into a yelp. Fuck.

"Ah, no more time for talky-talky. Just sucky-sucky? I didn't even get dinner first." Another bite on my opposite hip, this one tearing as he jerks his head to the side. I scream. After I recover, I go back to the snark. "I'm not usually this easy, you know." Another bite on my chest, then another on my neck right next to my mating mark. He bites repeatedly, only drawing a single mouthful from each one. Trying to make this as painful as possible. I've been hanging too long. My chest is starting to hurt, and I can't take a full breath, even without the screaming.

"Hide behind this blasé façade all you want, human. Your blood spills the same. I wonder if I can tear enough of your skin to remove your mark. It won't remove the bond, fortunately, but you'll be able to feel my marks on you every time you think of your mate." He proceeds to do just that. Tearing into my neck and shoulder like a rabid dog with a rabbit, shaking his head back and forth.

I can't fight it, just swinging like a marionette from the chains. When I pry my eyes back open, I look to gauge Ivan's face. He seems unconcerned, almost disinterested, but his mouth twitches occasionally like he's about to say something. I wish he would, but I can't count on Ivan not being a giant dick too. I think I've seen flashes of concern, but it could just be my mind clinging to hope, seeing things that aren't there.

A different kind of pain accompanies a popping sound. My hands and arms have long gone numb, so I wasn't anticipating more of it. I've actually lowered about an inch. I must be going into shock, which doesn't seem to line up with Constantine's plans. I can't breathe.

"Ugh, now you're truly damaged. Ivan! Get him down but don't unchain him. He's weak, but I don't want him getting too comfortable. Don't let him die; slow the bleeding from the biggest wounds."

Ivan gives a short nod and steps forward, grabbing my legs. He lifts a little bit at a time, moving slow enough to avoid injuring me further. Even with his surprising gentleness, I can't hold back my screams. Each bit of pressure taken off my wrists and shoulders feels like I'm being torn apart. The pain from the bites seems secondary, but it doesn't actually fade.

Feeling returns to my hands, none of it pleasant. People would describe it as something mundane when they'd walk after their leg fell asleep. This is not that. Pinpricks? No. Having the skin flayed from my hands to my back with a butter knife? Absolutely.
Ivan still makes no sound, holding me up with one arm under my ass and unclasping the chain from the hook in the ceiling. When my arms drop forward, he grabs them to slow the process.

Finally lowering me to the filthy cot, he brushes my hair out of my eyes. To check pupil dilation? He gently rubs me down like you would an overworked horse. I can see him doing these things, but it's like it's happening to someone else. No noise filters in. I still can't get a full breath.

My vision swims and I smile, knowing I'll go dark again soon. I need to come to accept that Ari might not make it in time. I don't know what happened to me just now, but I feel my body giving up. I know hanging for too long can cause suffocation, read it in an obscure online forum, I think. I'm glad something tore so at least I haven't died, but I won't make it another day at this rate. Ivan puts pressure on my neck and hip, the two biggest wounds at the moment.

My mind drifts to Ari. His life isn't directly tied to mine; he won't die with me. The bond is still there even if it's not as strong. Hopefully I didn't broadcast every pain I've felt today. Since I can't feel his emotions strongly right now, I'd call it a safe bet that I didn't. If he felt my pain all day, there's no way he'd still be sleeping or calm.

My eyes closed at some point, so I don't know if I'm alone, but part of me hopes Ivan is still here. I thought I'd never be alone again, having found my mate. I know he'll find me eventually; he'll never stop looking . . . I just want to be alive when he does.

A vision of us in front of a fireplace, snuggling under a blanket, fills my mind. His grunted response to my teasing, the tender looks he gives when he thinks I'm doing something especially adorable, like pestering his friends. It's all I ever wanted. A tear spills, tracking down my temple to my hairline. I just want my demon to hold me one more time.

Chapter Thirteen

Aridam

Murmuring voices wake me, the smell of coffee lingering. I push my top half off the table I slept on, blinking away the last remnants of sleep from my eyes. While I stretch my arms above my head, my back pops like I'm an old human. I don't feel anything from Rhys that would indicate he's awake, but Wrath prowls under my skin, extremely agitated. I shake off the feeling; there isn't time to fight with him.

Checking who is in the room, I see Lily. The moon casts light on her skin, and I struggle for a second to get a good look at her. She looks awful, like she hasn't slept. Her left hand grips a broken statue. I'm assuming it's the thing from Constantine's house that her friend retrieved. Her scrying crystal lies on a map in front of her on a long chain. Her head bowed, I know she's found nothing.

"We need to track down any remaining coven and get information. He could have a dozen more safe houses across the country." Belial speaks from the hall, looking up hopefully at Drystan. They're the two who have been the most vocal about finding my mate. Wrath thrashes again, harder to push down this time.

Azvameth slinks into the room, covered in filth and blood. He throws down a handful of severed fingers, blood splattering the map. "Did that. We got nothing, and we're running out of members."

I'm a little stunned. I had no idea he had even tried to help after I yelled at him yesterday, and torture is never his go-to. I look outside again. It's night, so I have no idea how long I slept. Too long, judging by how much work the team has done.

Alarm snakes through me. Did Rhys not wake up that whole time? I close my eyes to look inside myself, searching for the solid golden glow of our bond. My heart drops through my stomach as I take a good look. It's frayed, greying around the edges. I still feel nothing from him, but the bond flashes brighter for a second, showing he's awake. Why can't I feel him? There's not a way to block extreme emotion; it's a safeguard for mates to know when their bonded is in danger. There's something really wrong about how it's behaving.

The bond's corded light softens even more, becoming less solid. Numbness spreads through my chest, my heart seizing as I realize what I'm seeing. Wrath's agony hits me full force. He's been trying to get my attention for a while, for this. The bond is dying. An anguished sound rips from me, making the room go silent. I can feel stares but can't open my eyes. I'm staring at the bond, trying to grab on to it. I push as much reassurance and love as I can at it. Nothing.

"He's running out of time." I frantically look at my team. "We need Astaroth NOW!"

Belial presses a button on his headset, walking away quickly. Drystan rushes to hold me up as my knees buckle. "Hold it together, Aridam. Don't give up yet." He drags me to the sofa, setting me down. His whispered reassurances filter through my mind. I sense more movement around the room but can't bear to look up.

"Astaroth will join us shortly. He's calling in one of his favors from the angels. We'll find your mate, Aridam." Kieran steps as close as he dares. Wrath is unpredictable right now, ready to lash out at everyone.

"He's dying, Drys. The bond is dying; I can see it. I can't feel him anymore." I'm rambling, but I can't seem to stop. Until we hear from Astaroth, there's not much else we can do. I return to staring at our bond, trying to monitor how he's doing.

- - -

"Let's go! He said to meet us at the vamp's estate." Belial opens a portal and grabs my wrist, yanking me up to follow him. It's only been a few hours, but the bond has shown so much wear. It's barely visible, even to me.

Wrath hasn't lost hope yet, but he's hanging on by a thread. Insanity has a few hooks in him already. If we don't make it in time, I don't know that he will survive the death of his mate with any of his already questionable sanity intact.

Stumbling through, I stop when he does and look at our duke. He's standing next to Zadkiel, the angel of righteousness, and Raphael, the angel of healing. Their faces are all grim.

Zadkiel steps forward first. "I will track the soul of your mate, but I need to use your mate bond to do so. You'll have to open your heart and mind to me completely, demon, or I won't succeed."

"Anything," I croak. "Thank you. I know you have no stake in this, but I truly thank you." I've never been overly fond of angels, but I have no ill will toward these high-level light bringers. They cast no judgement on high-level demons; it's a nice change from the amount of hate spewed our way from others of their realm.

They both nod. Zadkiel steps forward until we're chest to chest. He places a large hand on either side of my face, drawing me forward. My first instinct is to push him away; Wrath is wriggling around, lashing out at me. Zad's eyes turn white, his gaze boring into mine. I feel him slip into my mind, and I follow. He flips through my life quickly, seeing it as Wrath and I did. He doesn't flinch at the things we've done. No contempt shown at the red haze or the death that follows me on assignments.

He stops at the day I met Rhys, watching carefully. Skipping again to the day I brought Rhys to Lily's. He gives a soft smile at my mate in my memory when he loses his cool and yells at me. His eyes look tender again when he watches Rhys hug Belial. Our sexual exploits are glossed over, to my relief, just pausing on the moment the bond snapped into place. He reaches into the memory and grabs the solid bond. I grunt at the feel of someone touching it besides my mate and me. After a few minutes, he releases the gold cord in my mind at the same time he lets go of my face physically.

He steps back, face drawn in sorrow. "Such a beautiful soul, your mate." I nod. He closes his pale eyes, moving them behind his lids.

"He's not far, maybe twenty miles from here. I'll bring you to the property he's being held at, but that's the most I can do. We cannot directly interfere. Raphael will be here waiting to heal what he can of your mate. I cannot tell you much, just that we have a very small window to save him."
I know that, but hearing it from an angel makes it more real. Rushing toward me, my team gathers around Zadkiel. Some are already in demon form, but I hold back, knowing I have less control of Wrath in that form.

We step through the angel's portal onto a flat field. A dilapidated house on a hill sits seemingly unguarded.
"Godspeed, demon." Rhys would have appreciated the irony and I would normally chuckle at the sentiment, but I will take whatever well wishes I can get. A nod from me and the portal closes. The guys, minus Kek and Dev, who haven't returned after collecting the souls, are ready to rip the place apart. A deep breath and I let go of the reins. Wrath bursts from me almost painfully, red haze already covering my vision. In a blur, we are on the porch of the house.

Belial cuts in front of me, opening the door, and blasts back. His scales give him a natural armor better than the thick demon skin the rest of us have. He writhes in pain on the ground, and while I can appreciate the sacrifice he made, Wrath doesn't even spare him a glance. Pushing through the door, we walk into an empty foyer. Kieran and Az rush in front of me, splitting up and tearing into the rooms. Each is empty. The house is clearly abandoned, and I worry we're too late.

A shout from the yard draws my attention, and I find Drystan pulling open a storm cellar door close to where Belial struggles to sit up. I can feel it in my gut; my mate is in there. I maneuver around Drys, slipping inside. It's dark enough that only a supernatural would be able to see. I don't bother trying to find a light. The room is empty, and Wrath lets out an enraged roar, at his wits' end. A scuff near a wall pulls at me. It looks like drag marks. The wall looks solid, but the longer I stare, the less it seems like a wall at all. The concrete looks off. Like a painting instead of a picture. Convincing but not the same.

Drystan pushes past me, making me growl my annoyance at my team repeatedly taking hits for me. He places his clawed grey hand on the wall, and it passes through with minimal effort. Showing his hand is unharmed by passing through the illusion, he waves me forward. Wrath pushes us through, gritting our teeth at the pain. It won't kill us, so we keep going. It's like walking through fiery quicksand. I finally stumble into a room of horrors. Blood is smeared throughout, and a tipped bucket pools more at my feet. My mate lays unconscious on a dirty cot, a vampire on each side. Constantine holds a knife to Rhys's throat, the blade digging into his skin with every shallow breath.

"Ah, how wonderful. Ivan, take over with the human, if you would. I would like to properly greet our guests." Constantine's tone is smug. I'm going to enjoy killing him.

They trade places seamlessly, leaving no opening for attack without signing Rhys's life away. Ivan's hand shakes a bit, taking the knife. His eyes are dead and his movements are jerky, like a robot almost. He's under compulsion. I would think it's impossible, but strong vampires can control the ones they sire, usually until they have control of their bloodlust. I want to use this to my advantage, but I don't know how yet without hurting my mate in the process.

"Your fellow demons don't have to hide. I know they're there. I can hear their blood singing." His tone is conversational, like he does this every day. My arms are sore; I'm holding my body so rigidly. Wrath doesn't acknowledge the vampire directly. He does make a few clicking noises, a warning to other predators that they need to flee an area. The fire in my gut burns hot, flames dancing under my skin.

"All right, since you don't seem to understand the situation, let me explain. He's your bonded, correct? Good, at least I'm talking to the right demon. Now, refuse to comply with my wishes? Your bonded dies. Attempt to harm me? Dies. If you're anything less than perfectly respectful to me and my efforts? He dies. I'm sure you see the pattern here."

"What do you want?" Wrath allows me to speak for us, sharing control.

"Simple. I want what every vampire wants. Power and blood. I was well on my way to finding the best blood sources. Alas, I don't have demon samples to compare. All I need is a few vials of your blood, plus a vial from each of your friends. See? Not too hard. You won't even feel it."

"That's it? You'll give me Rhys once you get the vials?" I know he's lying; he won't just give up the only thing keeping him alive. I spot Az moving so slowly I barely noticed him, making his way behind the trio in front of me.

Constantine laughs, a hollow sound conveying that he finds none of this funny. "No, I'll be keeping this little morsel for a while longer. He's simply delicious. I could keep him in this state for years, at the cusp of survival. It's touch and go right now, but if he survives the day, he'll survive being my personal blood pet. I'll treat him with as much kindness as he does me. Who knows? Maybe he'll grow to like it since I can't compel him to. Makes no difference to me."

Ivan's arm twitches again. Okay, I have a plan. I wrestle for full control. I need Wrath kept in check for this to work.

"Compulsion. That's something you do well, right? I mean, you'd have to, to control a vampire past their volatile transformation years. Ivan is, what, twenty? That's a gift a demon might have, not a vampire. Yet here we are. So I wonder . . . would your compulsion die with you?" I hope Ivan gets the message. His eyes show no recognition that I'm speaking, never mind what I'm saying.

"Ivan is a special breed—" That's all he manages to utter before his head is sliced clean from his body. Azvameth's claws drip with blood and brain matter, tossing the coven leader's head to the side.

Wrath demands to get his own hands bloody, pissed at being denied the chance to serve justice for his mate. Our wings jerk with his effort to attack the remaining vampire. Ivan's blade had cut into Rhys a little deeper in the millisecond before Constantine's demise, but he drops it now like it's on fire. Az notices my struggle and shields Ivan from our sight.

I force our eyes to Rhys, showing Wrath our mate. He immediately changes focus, rushing right along with me, passing Azvameth talking in hushed tones to Ivan. We make no move to go after the young vampire; I trust Az to get to the bottom of that clusterfuck. I reach Rhys, afraid to touch him. He's gaunt, bloody, and bruised. His chest only moves occasionally to breathe, maybe twice as slow as a normal human. I need to get him to Raphael.

I slide my arms under his limp form as carefully and quickly as I can. I try not to focus on his blood-covered body, clothes hanging off him in shreds. A portal opens, and I see Astaroth's head poke through. His anxious expression sets me on my nerves, but I speed over to him regardless, spotting our destination. In my haste I almost forget to create my own portal to take Rhys through but I manage without slowing too much. Stepping onto the now familiar courtyard, I set Rhys where my duke indicates. Raphael doesn't exchange pleasantries, not even an acknowledgment that I'm there. His sole focus is my sweet mate. His hands hover above his chest and glow a brilliant white.

I look inside myself to watch our bond. It's threadbare, blackened, and worn so badly, it's almost transparent. I had placed so much trust in the lifespan and accelerated healing that I didn't consider what would happen if it failed us. I still don't know what all was done to him, but his wounds were fatal several times over for a regular human. His neck is mottled with bites. The gouges seem to be focused over and around his mating scar, like a vampire tried to replace it or remove it entirely.

I watch it for what feels like hours, but the bond isn't improving. It's not working. I open my eyes to see the glow from the angel's hands fade. He turns to me.

"No," I deny.

"I'm sorry, Aridam. He's too far gone and magic isn't working."

"No! Fix him! FIX THIS! What good is being the angel of healing if you can't save him?! He's the best part of humanity, the best parts of me. He can't die!"

Wrath roars in denial and mourning, taking over completely, thrusting me violently to the side. There is no red haze, only heartbreak as he gathers our mate into our arms. Cradling his head to our neck, pressing our cheek to his, careful of our horns. He starts to beg.

"Please, mate. Stay. Keep safe. Keep fed. Mine. Stay." Tears track down our cheeks. I can hear sniffles from others, though I don't spare anyone a glance. My breath catches after every inhale my mate takes, paralyzed by the thought that each one will be his last. Wrath retreats, pushing me to talk to our mate.

"Sweet Rhys." I choke on a sob. "I love you; I've loved you since I saw you in that apartment. Don't leave me. I love you." I can no longer force anything to leave my mouth. I chant those three words in my head, holding my breath to keep the full-body shudders at bay. I push his hair away from his eyes, willing him to open them, to stay with me. I lean in to kiss his cracked lips gently, rocking him.

He takes the biggest breath he's had in hours, letting it out with a crackle, and stills. His heart beats three more times before stopping. The bond cracks, and pain like I've never felt rushes through my body. He's gone.

Chapter Fourteen

Rhys

I feel floaty and disjointed as I open my eyes. It's no longer hard to breathe; the pain has stopped. I watch the scene before me, trying to make sense of it. It's like looking through slightly foggy glass. Ari is hunched over a body, roaring into the estate yard. His posture is pure devastation. My heart breaks for him as I finally piece together that he's holding *me*. I step closer to my body and my mate, reaching to brush my hand across his cheek, but it passes through. If I had tears, I know I would be crying for him.

When he finally found me, I could hear what was going on but had been trapped in the darkest parts of my mind. I fought to get back to him with everything I had.

"I'm so sorry I wasn't stronger, big guy."

"You tried, Rhys James. That's more than most could say." The deep voice coming from my left surprises me. He's dressed like the man who tried to save me, except his white feathered wings and glowing aura make him unmistakable.

"Angel, right?"

A nod. "I'm Michael."

"Ah, makes sense. Angel of death." We stand and seem to wait for the other to speak. I don't know exactly what he wants from me right now.

"I'm sorry, Rhys, but we must go now. It's already been close to an hour since you passed." He reaches out his hand for me to take, and I stare at it.

"He doesn't deserve this, you know. To have his first mate reject him, then to have his second chance die in his arms so soon? It's not right. He's such a good man." I look back to where Ari is being pulled onto his feet by Drystan. Belial slips his arms under my body, holding me while Ari tries to get his shit together.

"And what about Belial? Giving him a twin soul before ripping it away? Peace for only a second? He's done nothing wrong."

"Sometimes things just don't work out. A lot of it doesn't make sense, but it's not our job to understand it."

I snort. "That's bullshit and you know it, Mikey boy. We are engineered to be curious, to try to find answers. Of course it's our job; it's one of the biggest truths of humanity." I can't take my eyes off Ari. His wings drooping, tail just hanging listlessly behind him.

"Can I stay with him a little longer? I need to know he'll be all right."

"What would you do with a second chance, Rhys? Cure cancer? Solve world hunger?"

I shake my head at his ludicrous question. "Nothing so grand. Honestly? Just love him. Be the best version of myself for him and those I care about. Sasha will be okay. She has Colin and she'll be able to recover. These two, though? I can only hope they push through and don't go back to being shells of themselves."

"You know you can still see him after you go through Reception, right? You can still be together, but he will no longer be your soulmate. Your soul will no longer belong to you once you enter The Three Gates."

"Yeah, I got that. It's why Astaroth is so frantic about his own mate. They didn't say it as plainly as you did, but I put two and two together." A deep breath before I utter some pretty damning words. "He will still have to grieve me as I am, Michael. Having to feel the hollow empty space our bond resided in in our chests forever? Every moment will fall short. Bittersweet almost. Funny thing, though? I'd do it all again the exact same way. Maybe jump him a little sooner—you have to admit that ass is mighty fine—but I'd do everything all over again just to have the moments we did."

"Second chances don't come around often, Rhys James."

"I know. Otherwise, reincarnation would be rampant. Time would warp and life would stop being as beautifully fragile." Look at me, being all philosophical with an angel. "Why did you bring up second chances, Mikey? You're going to fill a man up with hope and then just leave him hanging? You sly dog."

A wry smile curves his lips. "It's Michael."

"Answers, wingman, or I'll come up with worse."

"A recommendation came to me by another angel. Two, actually, Zadkiel and Raphael." He motions to the angel who had tried to save me. He looks so sad, watching my mate struggle.

"A second chance, Rhys James. You can appeal your death. You would have to give up a part of you, though. There's a kind of magic needed to send you back, and as a full Null, you aren't susceptible, even after death."
 "How do I appeal?" I ignore what he says about giving up a part of me. I'll deal with whatever it is.

"You simply ask. I am the angel of death, after all."

"Are you serious? Just ask? That's dumb. I mean . . . ahem, okay. Can I appeal my death with you, Michael?" He better not be joking.

167

"Yes, Rhys James."

I feel my stomach swoop as the world spins around me. We are now standing in what looks like the library from *Beauty and the Beast*. I panic for a second, hating not being able to see Ari. It must show on my face.

"Calm, Rhys. We are in a place unbothered by the passing of time. Being a Null doesn't absolve you from time and space. That's all this is. A pocket beyond those things. If you succeed, you will rejoin your mate in the same moment we left."

"Umm, so I have a few questions . . ." I doubt he knows what he's in for.

"Ask them now; I will not be able to help you once you start your appeal."

"What *is* my appeal, exactly? You're talking like it's a quest. What happens to my twin soul thing with Bel? I thought my being a Null was the only way I could be near him or any of them for a long period of time." I had more, obviously, but I'm trying to get the important ones out first.

"Your appeal is a trial of sorts. It's different for every being that goes through it, so I cannot tell you what yours will entail. I do know it's about choices and strength of heart. Zadkiel seems to think you can make it through. I don't know what you did to inspire such faith in you, but you have his."

I don't stop to think about it too long; I just want to get this over with.

"As for your other concerns." A pause. "How you interact with Belial will not change. As his twin soul, you will be able to push past the sin leaking from him. It's there but will feel tangible so you can identify the magic, similar to how you can now, and physically move it away from you. As for the others, I believe you will be a little more affected than you experienced before. Their influence will be significantly weaker, but you will still be susceptible to their sins' pull. You're giving up a piece of your soul, Rhys. It's not to be taken lightly. When you give up that piece of yourself, you give up your Choice at The Three Gates. When you die next time, you'll become a shadowling in Hell, skipping Reception altogether."

Well, shit. I mean, I'll take it; I just have to take significantly better care of myself. I square my shoulders. Any other questions I have fall to the wayside. I need to get back to my mate, my family.

"Okay, I'll figure the rest out later. I'm ready."

"Yes, I believe you are."

"Any last words of wisdom, Mikey boy?"

"Follow your heart, Rhys James, not just your mind. Don't second-guess yourself." Before I can give him sass for the cliché, he touches my forehead and the world goes dark. I didn't feel myself move, but the air feels different. I strain my eyes to see something, anything around me.

Like a horror movie, a small spotlight shines on a stage to my left, making me do a full-body turn in that direction. Standing under the strong blue-white glow is my mother. She has a smile and tears in her eyes. She looks exactly like her photos in the papers I hoarded as a child. I take a step forward, and she shakes her head. I tilt mine in confusion. "Mom?"

Another light shows myself with small angel wings and a serene face. I know it's supposed to depict where I would be going to be at peace, but I look like a tool. I roll my eyes, and the other me gives a small nod. Fucking angel? Really? I wait for a third light; this shit usually happens in threes, right? Nothing else happens. I start laughing. "Oh God, this is what I have to choose between? The mother who saved me and a weird version of myself?" I take another step toward my mom, and she gives another small shake of her head. The fuck?

"Am I missing something?" A nod. Her tears finally spill over, gliding down her face.

"What do I do?" No response. I look at angel me, and his face still looks so stupid and peaceful. I want to punch it.

"Okay, so it's not a you-or-becoming-an-angel thing. Is it both?" I look to her for an answer and receive a tiny nod.

"So I have to give you up too?" No, not when she's this close. When I can finally talk to her. I have so much I need to ask her, to feel a real mom hug for the first time. My heart cracks. I know I'll give her up, but I hate every bit of it.

"I love you, Mom, but I can't choose you." She smiles softly at me and nods, eyes wet.

One more. "You—fuckface." I point to angel me. His/my white wings ruffle. "I don't choose you."

He fades with that peaceful love-drunk look on his/my face. I sigh, thinking I'm done, but then a small demon version of me takes his place. I look like a badass. White skin with dark markings like Devland. Greed demon. I'm actually not surprised. The black marks are dense over my chest. If I chose this way, I could still have Belial and Ari in Hell. I wouldn't have to choose between them and my mom. She has neither wings, leather or feather, as far as I can tell, so I have no idea where she comes from. Could I give up my bond to Ari to keep my mom and all of my "not magic" magic? I feel a little like a greed demon already, trying to figure out how to keep it all. I wrestle for a long time with myself before remembering Michael's advice.

In the end, it isn't really hard to follow my heart instead of my head. I made the right choice the first time. I refuse to deny my mom again, but I can't choose her either. I realize this might keep going until I cave or I figure out the riddle. I just want my mate.

"I choose Aridam. I choose my mate," my voice rings out, unwavering.
 I don't know if I expected a grand finale kind of moment or what, but the soft fading of everything around me back into the library with Michael was not it.

"I thought I'd wake up if I succeeded? Also, that was like thirty minutes max. I thought it would be longer . . . and harder."

"You were gone for close to six hours, Rhys."

"Really? Fuck."

"It's normal for it to go on for days. Not everyone has such convictions, the Choice not as easy for most as you claim it is. Mothers joining their children, people choosing their mates who have already passed on."

"I understand. So I'm done?"

"You will return, Rhys. Just a little more patience."

I try to stand still, like I'm not chomping at the bit to get back to my mate. I'm failing miserably if Mikey's raised brow is any indication. He shakes his head ruefully. I watch as his eyes go white, and he steps up to me.

"We have to take a part of your soul, remember? So I can return you to your body."

Oh shit, that's right. "Sorry, I forgot. What do I need to do?"

"Truly want it gone and bear the pain of it ripping from you. It's going to be excruciating, similar to what ended your life before."

"Do it." I close my eyes, waiting.

"Relax, Rhys James."

I snort. *Well, why didn't you say so?* I roll my eyes under my lids but do really try to stay calm.

His hands land on my shoulders, pressing down. My knees almost buckle under the weight. A beat passes, and then a scream leaves my lips unbidden as the pain claws its way through my body, starting at my toes. My back bows as it travels up, passing through my legs to my core. It's not fast. The agony as it reaches my heart causes my body to convulse, and I collapse in slow motion. Michael's hands follow me to the ground, never leaving my shoulders. I grit my teeth so I won't bite off my tongue, if that can even happen as just a soul. The screaming continues even after I lose my voice, the silence almost worse. By the time the ripping feeling makes its way to my head, I'm lying locked like a statue. This pain is worse than dying, but I want it gone, want it done. The final rush leaves me, and I sob in relief. I don't feel the same, like my body isn't fully my own.

Michael's hands smooth up over my neck, grabbing my face. He leans in and presses our cheeks together. "You did so good, Rhys." I just whimper in response. "I need to go through your mind and watch your life with your mate to help you back into your body. Zadkiel did this with Aridam to find you. You'll be able to watch with me in your mind; you don't have to open your eyes or move."

I grunt my acceptance, bracing myself for more pain. Instead, a screen of sorts appears, and my life speeds past on it, stopping at the day I mated Aridam. It speeds up again, rushing through most of my time as Constantine's pincushion, pausing at the moment I knew the bond was fading. I watch the tear slide out of my eye, but Michael watches my chest where I see our bond glowing faintly. He grabs ahold of it, making it flash brightly. He keeps his grip tight as time moves forward again. We watch as Wrath begs me to stay, and my chest pangs when I remember the devastation in my demon's voice. He continues to hold the bond as time passes again, until right before the bond breaks. My last inhale.

Slowly, I come back to myself. I feel his hands leave my face, but keep my eyes closed. Silence stretches for a moment, and I'm tempted to try to open them just to see what he's doing.

"Are you ready, Rhys? It's going to be a long road to recovery. All the pain you felt while dying will still be there when you wake up."

"Yes, please, Mikey boy. Take me back to my mate."

My stomach dips again, and I feel motion sick. Breathing like I'm in a Lamaze class seems to help, though why it does when I don't actually breathe as a dead guy totally fucks me up.

"You'll feel a push and pull, and then you only have to focus on opening your eyes. Fight for the life your heart wanted so badly, Rhys James, and Godspeed."

I snicker. He's funny when he wants to be.

A shove is too light a word; I don't feel a little push or pull. I'm picked up and body slammed back into my physical body. A breath whooshes into my lungs, filling them to capacity.

A yell escapes my lips as the pain returns like a freight train. Everything hits me all at once. I feel like I'm drowning in sensation. The arms I'm being carried in almost drop me, Belial's intake of air loud and sharp.

I feel his sin's magic pulsing along my skin, but I brush it away with a limp flick of my wrist and a thought. I set my hand back down on his chest, patting gently. There's so much going on inside of me that I can't focus, but touching him seems to help calm my mind. I know he's talking, but I'm not retaining anything.

My mate bond snaps back into place once I go looking for it, glowing bright gold in my mind's eye. A black sliver the width of a needle winds its way through the length of it. I don't get to examine it for very long. Their combined emotions start to pummel me, battering my heart so that it matches my body. The grief is overwhelming.

Shouting erupts as I crack my eyes open, finding Wrath's face and focusing my attention solely on my mate. He looks frozen, like he might be going crazy.

"Hey, big guy," I croak. It's lame, but that's all I got.

His eyes widen, the beautiful silver swirl stilling, Ari coming front and center. I give a small smile, lip cracking and bleeding as a result. That seems to snap him out of it. He rushes to me like a linebacker, ripping me out of Belial's arms and crushing me to his chest. I don't tell him to stop, because he knocked the wind out of me, but I feel the moment my pain hits him. His hands immediately gentle. He cradles me against his chest like something precious, kissing my lips so softly, tears start to fall.

"Oh, sweet Rhys. I love you, I need you. Please never leave me again." His whispered words become a mantra; he's repeating them so reverently.

I bring my hand up to cup his cheek, the effort making my arm shake. "I love you too, my mate. I need you to do me a favor, though, okay?"

"Anything."

"Let the angel of fucking healing come closer so he can fix me with his magic glow-y hands, yeah?" I spotted Raphael when Ari had jerked me from Belial. He's hovering right outside of Wrath's considerable reach, looking fondly at us.

"I'm so sorry, baby, of course." It takes him a second. "It won't work, though, Rhys. You're a Null. I'll take you home, we'll let you rest, and then we can figure out what happened." I scoff at him and turn my head to Raphael. My vision dims a little at the stupid move, but I keep going.

"Give me the glow-y hands, Mr. Sexy Healer Man! Apparently my mate doesn't feel like listening today. I'll forgive him; he's had a rough few hours." I think I wink at him, letting everyone know I'm just trying to rile up and distract my mate. It might have been a blink or a constipated face, though. I can't tell.

I know Ari needs some answers, but my pain level is fucking crazy. I plead in my head for the angel man to hurry the fuck up. Raph finally takes those last steps to me, his kind eyes twinkling. This time, where he hovers, his hands feel warm and tingly, and I can feel my skin stitching together. My aches and pains practically disappear over the course of the next few minutes. He sags against me, careful not to touch Ari at all. I pat his hand and thank him.

"All right, big guy, there's a lot I need to tell you guys, but I'd rather not get into it in the middle of Captain Crazy Pants' yard. Can we go back to Lily's?" I motion to the angel still standing there. "Raphael, you and Zadkiel should come too."

I notice quite a few absences from the team but can't think of where they might be. I'm not tracking well.

I rest my eyes as the guys talk logistics, and let the scent of my mate wash over me.

Chapter Fifteen

Rhys

My eyes struggle to open, and I'm thrown back into that storm cellar, memories assaulting me. I thrash against the weight pressed against me. I'm terrified to open my eyes, but I'm finally able to force them. I see Constantine looming over me, my blood dripping down his chin. He grabs my wrists and I scream, fighting his hold. I remember Kek telling me to fight vampires as much as possible, to keep my wrists and neck away from them if I can. My demon will come for me. I can almost hear his voice soothing me.

Constantine abruptly releases me, talking to someone in the room. Probably Ivan. That poor man never said a word to me, but his eyes told me a story anyway. I had a lot of time to stare at him while Constantine held me, and I don't think he agreed with my treatment but never helped me other than a kind touch while doctoring me up occasionally.

I can still hear my mate's voice in soft tones. I can't make out the words, concentrating too hard on the crazy vamp in front of me. He turns back, and I see his mouth moving. What is he saying?

"You're okay, sweet Rhys, I love you. He's dead, baby. Come back to me."

Constantine's mouth and Ari's voice sync up. The pale boy-band look-alike fades, blond hair darkening to black. Ari's face replaces his and I recoil. Is this a trick? The fuck? I close my eyes and search for my mate bond. It's bright, the black vein reminding me of the past twenty-four hours. Memories flood me, and I launch myself at my mate the second my eyes open again.

"I'm so sorry, so sorry, so sorry." I'm wracked with guilt for thinking even for a second that my mate was that monster. I'm sobbing, blubbering out my waking nightmare, begging him to understand.

Ari wraps himself around me, lowering us to the bed. He murmurs his forgiveness. I know I don't deserve it, but I'll take it. Once I'm able to get myself under control, I notice Bel by the door. I hate that he witnessed my breakdown, but if it were anyone other than my mate, I'm glad it was him.

Belial is pale, his eyes rimmed with red. I haven't been able to really look at him until now. I open my mouth, but he turns away quickly and rushes out of the room. I can't help but feel hurt.

"He's struggling, baby. He portals in to check on you every hour for a few minutes before leaving. He's cut contact with everyone but you and me."

My heart breaks for my friend. I was so focused on reassuring Ari and resting that I didn't explain what happened. I know how your imagination can be a million times worse than reality. I know how something like this would eat at him.

"Do you feel okay now, baby? Do you need anything?"

"Umm. I could probably eat something. I do need to talk to the team, though, and the angels."

"That's fine. I sent them home when you slept for more than a few hours, but we can call them back anytime. We'll have them meet us here in . . . say, two hours?"

"Perfect." I cup his cheek. "Kiss?"

"Always." It's over way sooner than I'd hoped, just a gentle meeting of the lips.

"No hanky-panky?" I pout. "You better not be withholding that demon dick under some misguided idea that I need more rest. I need dicked down, big guy."

A chuckle bursts from my mate, his eyes widening in surprise. This might be the first time he's laughed since I was taken. He tries to give me a reproachful look, but his eyes crinkle with humor.

"I'll verify with the angel that you're all healed up. Then we'll spend a whole day in bed, my mate, I promise." I get another sweet kiss before he hauls me off to the bathroom. Good idea! I'd kill for a bath right now, and I have to reek. I give my armpit a cursory sniff and recoil. That's awful. How did he cuddle me with that stench?

He doesn't release me, just sits on the edge of the giant clawfoot tub, turning the water on and adding . . . is that bath oil? Smells relaxing, like lavender. Steam rises from the water, and Ari slowly undresses my top half, the bond pinging with pain at each yellow bruise and pink scar he reveals. I move to stand, needing to see them for myself too.

I realize I haven't so much as looked in the mirror since I've been back. After I strip completely, I continue to avoid looking in the mirror. For whatever reason, I don't want to see my neck most of all. I know it's littered with bites and evidence that Constantine tried to remove my mark by repeatedly biting through it. Looking down, my eyes focus on every bite and slash. The bruising looks gnarly but will fade within a few days. The scar tissue covering me will not. A few are neat pinpricks, just two evenly spaced dots, clustered around my torso. Others look like a chunk was taken out.

I trace my right hip where the largest scar resides on my front. A small fistful of muscle and fat is gone, leaving a noticeable dip, almost like a shark bite. It echoes with the pain I felt with every chunk he tore from me. I remember goading him, this being my punishment. I shudder. I want to hide my new and definitely not improved body from my mate, but he brushes each spot reverently, pushing my hand gently away from my hip. I don't feel revulsion from him, but I'm sure he can feel it from me. He leans down and kisses the scar I was tracing, licking around the edges. It's not meant to be sexual, but my dick rises to the occasion anyway. We both ignore it, choosing to keep the mood soothing. He leans over to flick the water off before it overflows, eyes not leaving my body.

My legs are a mess; crisscrossing scars cover most of my calves and thighs. My knees and ankles seem to have been mostly left alone. I even have marks on my toes. They're razor thin, reinforcing my belief that they were done while I was unconscious. I remember seeing most before now, on that first day. It wasn't this extensive, though. I feel violated, used, dirty. I don't recall a lot of my time there; what else did they do to me in my sleep? I feel like I would have felt the effects of any penetration, so I push it from my mind. Angel man might have an idea, but I honestly don't want to know.

Ari turns me around, sucking in a breath. "Oh, baby." He sounds teary, which cranks up my anxiety.

"What?! Is it bad? How ugly is it?"

"Not ugly, my mate. You're so strong. It's . . . there's . . . fuck! There's more scarring on your back." He struggles to get the words out. "Baby, they . . . they carved a symbol into your skin. Constantine's emblem. It's not wholly correct; the scarring distorts it a little."

I feel faint and nauseous, my panicked hands flapping. Definitely wins the battle for weird reactions. "Fuck, I need to see it." I try to turn to see, but he's trying to hold me still. "Let me look!" I pull out of his grip with quite a lot of effort. Using the mirror to look at my back, I skip checking my face and neck entirely. Between my shoulder blades, where Ari normally holds me down while we mess around, is the rough image of a long vertical dagger with a large "C" carved over the top two thirds. The curve of the letter is a little wonky, but it's unmistakable. My knees grow weak, and I can't look any longer. I stare instead at the ground in front of my toes, waiting for Ari to figure out what to do next. I'm done. Tapped out.

He gently takes my hand, careful not to touch my wrists, knowing it seems to trigger me. He leads me to the edge of the tub and dips my fingers in, giving me time to protest if the water is too hot. It's not. I want it as hot as possible to scrub the vampires' touch from my skin. It still freaks me out that this body was dead, like dead-dead, for a few full minutes before Michael hulk-punched me back to life.

He lowers me into the bath, my legs too unsteady to try to step over the tub's edge. The water is already turning pink. I'm able to look up as my mate climbs in behind me, pulling me partially into his lap. My back rests lightly against his front. I can feel the sensation of his skin rubbing my scars with every inhale. He leans into my space, leaving small kisses along my neck.

"We'll figure out a way to remove it, sweet Rhys, I promise."

I believe him. We do know a few angels and witches, after all. Even if it stays forever, it's a reminder that I succeeded in coming back. I'm able to come to terms with it pretty quickly, but Ari is not.

"I'm so sorry you went through this. It's because of me. Because I brought you into this world. You could still be at your apartment, having coffee dates with your friend and living a carefree life. Not *dying* and being tortured because you fell in love."

"Oh, shove it, mate. I'd do it again in a heartbeat if it meant staying with you." I flush at my own cheesy line, but Wrath's purring makes my embarrassment worth it.

Ari squirts some of our shampoo into his hand after wetting my hair. The massaging circles make me melt, and any resistance I still carried floats away. He rinses my hair carefully and does a second wash. I'm glad he seems to feel my need to be squeaky clean. After it's all rinsed out, he slathers on entirely too much conditioner. It's endearing, though; he had never used conditioner before we got together. To my horror, he was a body wash and hair combo kind of guy—if he showered at all. Apparently quick dips in Hell's lakes are "refreshing."

He grabs a soft cloth from the side of the tub and squirts some of my new body wash on it. It smells exactly like the one in my apartment. Like sandalwood and leather with just a hint of vanilla. He makes sure to get every nook and cranny twice. I don't know if my belly button has ever been so fresh. I giggle as he scrubs behind my ears and down my neck. His delight flashes through the bond, and I smile. He's trying so hard. Gah, I love him. I wait patiently for him to rid me of the massive amounts of conditioner before I straddle his thighs and hug him to me. I whisper my declaration of love, knowing I don't have to be loud for him to hear me. I get the murmured words back, and I bask in the feeling of being safe and with my mate.

He doesn't rush me, but I know we're going to be cutting it close on time before everyone gets here. I peel myself off of Ari and climb out, drying myself off while telling him to finish his bath or maybe just shower instead.

"The water looks gross now, big guy. You shouldn't be washing in dirty water. I'll even rinse off again myself before we go to bed tonight, okay?" I get a grunt in response, and I can't help but chuckle at his default grumpy setting.

Drifting back to our room, I rummage in Ari's drawers. We've kind of taken over and moved into this room way more than normal visitors would, but I'm happy we did. I find a collared shirt of Ari's, and it's big enough to just work as a nightgown and still cover my neck. I feel ridiculous, but his scent is still lingering and it's not like anyone will make fun of me. I try to find pants, but all I have are tight jeans and basketball shorts that won't cover up my scars anyway. Where did my sweats go? Maybe Lily took them, sneaky witch.

I'm still standing at the dresser, staring at the jeans, when Ari joins me. His arms wrap around my waist, not shying from my damaged hip. His deep inhale tells me he approves of my attire.

"You better not be only grabbing pants because you want to hide your legs, mate." His voice is a dangerous growl.

"I don't want anyone to see, Ari. It's bad enough you have to look at them."

"I just want you to be comfortable, and jeans are going to chafe against your skin, especially your hip."

"I'll take a little chafing right now. It's better than walking around in just a shirt, long as it is. My briefs will rub right on the big one, so I do need something to cover my disco balls. I was never excited about showing off my body before all this, so I'm not changing, like, a core part of my personality."

A sigh shows I win. "Okay, sweet Rhys. Would you like help getting them on?" His voice is almost hopeful.

I chuckle. "Nah, I got it. You get dressed too."

- - -

Walking into the meeting room, I draw up short, making Ari almost knock into my back. Astaroth is standing opposite Zadkiel, having some sort of silent stare-off. Z cracks first, shaking himself off. I don't know what started it, but they seem to be trying to pretend it never happened. I wonder if I'm missing something.

No matter. Ari finds us a seat, and I climb into his lap, settling down. I wave to the few demons already seated.

"Are the others all coming later?"

"We didn't know how you would react being around Kek and Devland right now."

"Why?"

"Because they didn't protect you! They didn't listen to me over the comms, so focused on going through the empty fucking room that they ignored me yelling that you were not alone, that you needed help!" Bel appears in front of me in his demon form, looking like he's lost all control. His green scales almost shimmer in his anger. He looks like an angry dragon man with no wings.

I need to soothe him. "Oh, Bel. That must have been awful. I'm so sorry you went through that."
"Me?! You're sorry for me?! Be angry, Rhys. Those vampires never would have gotten to you if Kek and Devland had cared to do anything but listen to their sins. I can't see either of them right now or I'll rip them apart." His chest heaves.

I stand and proceed to climb my twin, wrapping myself around him. His arms automatically hold me up. "Shh, it's okay. You told me to wait for the guys. You all asked me not to leave the protection of the demons, and I didn't listen. I thought being a Null and mated to a demon made me more invincible than it did. It's no one's fault, Bel-Bel. You can't blame yourself or anyone else, other than a guy who is already super dead."

His shoulders drop, and I feel the envy that had been swirling around the room dissipate a fraction. I allow myself to be pulled off of him and tucked into Ari's side. Wrath is riding him hard, but I'm glad Ari still has control. I take a wild guess at what has him so upset. "You can't kill your team, big guy. It's not their fault."

"I'm trying, mate." I love being in Ari's arms. Even when he's enraged and barely controlled, he treats me like glass. Well, outside of the bedroom.

I look around again. "Okay, but where's Az?" I wanted to thank him.

"He's otherwise engaged, dear boy. I applaud you being so concerned with the whereabouts of my demons, but we do have precious little time. We would like to start with you and what happened when you were taken. I know it will be difficult for you to tell us everything, but every detail matters." Astaroth's tone is probably meant to be soothing. It missed the mark just a tad. "Aridam, will you be able to control yourself? It might be best if you sit this one out." I know the duke is just baiting him, but Ari seems to take it seriously.

"Do not try to separate us now, sir. I've seen the evidence on his body. I need to account for every scar, and I need to do so while holding my mate." I pat his arm and motion for him to sit so I can take my normal seat in his lap.

Once everyone is settled, I explain everything that I remember from the moment I left the guys at the estate until my death. I try to keep my face blank and my voice toneless, factual. I slip up in spots, normally when thinking about the bond and how damaged it became in such a short time. I gloss over the feelings I had but make sure to be meticulous with every word Constantine had spoken and every time Ivan seemed to disagree with Constantine's orders. When I'm done, I receive a nod from the duke. Ari's arms had wrapped tighter and tighter around me as my story went on.

"That's, um . . . actually not all. Gah, how do I start this?" I look at the angels sitting at the back of the room. Raphael's eyes are suspiciously wet, and Zadkiel's are carefully blank. "I need to thank you. Both of you. It's true that without you, my mate wouldn't have found me in time. I mean, I guess he still didn't, 'cause I died." I pat Ari's arm as he crushes me against him. "When you prayed for me to get a second chance, it reached Michael. He was waiting for me after I died. He said it was because of you two that I could appeal my death. So, thank you. I'd never met either of you, and you had so much faith in me. I can't tell you what that means."

"We're so glad you made it through your appeal and were able to rejoin your mate almost fully intact. It's truly a testament to how much you love your mate," Raphael says.

"What do you mean almost fully intact?" Ari demands.

I sigh, not really wanting to explain in front of everyone, but at this point, they've heard everything else. "I had to give up part of my soul and part of my Null magic to return." I glower at Zadkiel when he opens his mouth like he's going to contribute to my explanation. My mate doesn't need to know how painful it was.

I turn fully in Ari's arms and cup his face. "I'd do it again in a heartbeat, and I'll tell you everything else later."

Astaroth interrupts our tender moment. "Oh, dear boy, you've given us a small clue we hadn't even considered until now. Only an angel can remove pieces of a soul. Is that correct, Zadkiel?"

"That I know of. Only high-level angels have the ability, and it's some, not all."

"So how are the shredded souls appearing at Reception? Only an angel could damage a soul like that. You and I both know high-level angel doesn't mean pure and good. Just as a high-level demon doesn't mean evil. How many high-level angels are you guys up to now? A hundred? That's truly not many compared to the couple thousand Hell has. You might need to gather the heavy hitters and make sure you can account for them and their motives. I'm taking this matter to Gabriel tomorrow, so you may want to hurry."

Both angels disappear in a blink, slightly panicked looks on their faces.

"Who is Gabriel? I mean, I know archangel, blah, blah, blah. But who is he really?"

"He's my counterpart in Heaven. I'm the duke of demons in their first cycle. I'm responsible for the actions of the high-level demons, and the low-level after orientation. The low-level demons are easy enough since Hell technically owns them. I can just start their transition into shadowlings if they step out of line. There's another duke, Allocer, who is in charge of them then. A third duke, Mammon, is in charge of the souls once they enter The Three Gates until they are fully transitioned and trained. He tosses all the really bad eggs straight to Allocer so I don't have to deal with them.

"Now, Gabriel is the Commander of the Angels. He oversees every high- and low-level angel. His fellow commanders, Azrael and Chamuel, take care of the rest. They don't really have cycles like Hell does. Heaven is run on prayer, not shadowlings, so low-level angels just get to be guardian or helper angels forever unless they totally fuck up. Does that answer some of your questions, dear boy?"

"That was amazing." My voice is breathy. I know part of me being horny at his response is having been close to Kieran for this long, but Astaroth answering all my questions before I even ask them is crazy hot. Ari growls deep in his chest, not liking what he's feeling through the

bond. I turn in his lap again and put on my best puppy eyes. Chuckles erupt behind me, but I pay no mind.
 "Bed?"

I know he enjoys my one-word requests, maybe even better than my rambling questions. He wastes no time, tossing me over his shoulder and running back to our room, where he proceeds to show me with his mouth exactly who I belong to.

Chapter Sixteen

Aridam

It's hard to remember that Rhys isn't actually attracted to any of the team or our duke. I know Kieran gets to him the most right now. Considering what he told me about his appeal when he was . . . away, I can see Devland being really hard for him to be around for long periods of time too, since he's already shown greed as being the sin he identifies with the most. Wrath sulked a little when we found out, but once our sweet mate explained that greed and wrath go together better than two wraths, he was mollified.

After all our orgasms last night, I shouldn't be this distracted, but I'm finding it hard to focus on the updates we're getting.

"The Albany Alpha is in the wind. The whole pack is in chaos. We have to track him down, but with half the team not here, I don't know what to do." Bel sounds more stressed than usual. I know he's been taking the Rhys situation hard, but I think he hates being at odds with any of the team just as much. It doesn't seem to matter that they've apologized to him over and over; he's holding his grudge.

They haven't attempted face-to-face contact with me yet, but I know it'll happen soon. The voice messages and texts helped quell my anger a little. They sound wrecked. I now have Wrath convinced they don't need to die, so we're compromising on how much maiming will happen. I've been told Azvameth is actually going to be helping with questioning Ivan and tracking the remaining members of the coven. There's something going on there, but I'm content to wait until Az is ready to talk.

"Bel, why don't we send someone to track the alpha? It can be delegated to a low-level demon. There's no reason to have the whole team out for one rogue wolf. We keep monitoring all his activities online and interfere if necessary."

"You're right; I just don't like this being a loose end."

"Have you talked to anyone but me today? Maybe we can both go see the angel therapist Astaroth suggested. I admit I was hesitant, but Rhys agreed to go and asked that I go with him and to have my own sessions. I agreed." He definitely threatened to "chop off my nuts since he doesn't need them as much as my dick," and that may have had a significant weight in my decision, but Bel doesn't need to know that.

I continue. "It's not healthy for you or the team to be so torn up and throwing blame around. At least talk to Rhys.

Ask him to hang out; you know he would love to see you more. It's been easier for me to process because of him."

"I'll do that." He won't.

"I see you're being stubborn. Fine. We need to have a team meeting, Bel. Either get over it or get help. Now."

I hate using tough love on Bel. It's the only thing that seems to work sometimes, but I feel like shit every time I raise my voice. I walk to the kitchen and find myself alone with Lily.

"We'll be out of your hair soon, I promise."

"Take your time. You guys have a lot going on, and if Rhys feels safe here, he should stay as long as he wants. Have you figured out a way for him to go home with you yet? Or are you making the move up here?"

Shit. I haven't even thought about it.

She scoffs. "Men. Don't you think he would like having a place to call home? At this point, I've had all his things moved to storage and his apartment was given up. His phone is current, but he's missed hundreds of calls from someone named Sasha, and the NYPD. I can only assume she's the one who reported him missing with how long it's been since they've talked." She leans forward. "Don't let his life be swallowed up by yours, demon. He's jumped headfirst into this very new world for you, but he needs to keep hold of the things that make him happy from his old life. His best friend being one of them."

I feel awful. What kind of mate am I that I've never even asked about his best friend? Until now, I didn't know he gave up his lease or that he was paying for storage. It didn't even occur to me to ask. He was so proud of that tiny shithole of a place, and I didn't think twice about it.

My mate tears into the room, on high alert. "I can feel your worry and sadness, Ari. What's going on? Is everyone okay?"

"Oh, sweet Rhys, I'm so sorry. I've neglected you as my mate."

"Huh?"

"Your apartment, your storage unit, your job, your friends?! How could I have not noticed you weren't completely happy?"

"Why would you think I wasn't happy? Yes, I need to call Sasha, but I wanted to do it when this was over so you could come with me to meet her. I'm not upset about the apartment or anything else. I made peace with losing my job weeks ago, big guy. In case you've forgotten, we've been kind of busy."

"You've been reported missing, Rhys."

He chuckles. "Let me call her real quick so she can end the dramatics." My mate saunters out, like having a person report you missing isn't a huge deal.

I try to give him some time, but an hour later when I go in search of him, he's still on the phone with Sasha. I can tell by his relaxed stance and soft smile that he's okay. She's rambling along, and I find it fascinating that in this friendship, *he's* the quiet one.

"Babe, I gotta go. Ari's here and we need to make dinner. Stop stressing. I'm sorry I'm a bitch, and I'll see you for coffee next Monday!" He hangs up and tosses his phone to the table. He stalks toward me with a smile on his face.

"Okay, maybe you're right. I forgot how much I missed her with all the crazy shit going on. I'll meet her for coffee in a few days and call her again tomorrow. Hey, would you come too? To coffee?"

"Of course, baby. I would love to meet your friend. Did you want to stop by the club and see anyone while we're out?" It's not a huge walk from one shop to another, but I feel like it's in a weird spot. I'd rather portal.

"Yes, please!" His smile reassures me this is the right move. I need to start looking at properties.

- - -

Another day has passed, but we are no closer to getting information. Azvameth is still suspiciously absent. I know he's been on assignment, but he's not giving us updates via text or stopping by. There's something going on with him, but I cannot dwell on it. Today will be a day of reckoning for other members of my team.

I'm in the living room of the team house in Hell, waiting for Kek and Devland to show up. They haven't reached out, and the unease in the team needs to stop. I'll beat their asses and then we'll move on . . . hopefully. Drystan has accompanied me in case Wrath gets out of hand and they need help with a portal out.

The first to walk through is Kek. His eyes are bloodshot and his face is drawn. A twinge of guilt runs through me, but punishment needs to be dished out. His pride won't let him admit he was wrong, but he seems to be torn up about it. It'll be cathartic for both of us. His eyes harden, but I catch the flash of relief. Wrath pushes forward and leaps over the couch, on him before he can say anything.

After a few punches, Wrath realizes he isn't fighting back. It takes some wind out of his sails but doesn't stop him from bloodying the pride demon. Devland hasn't returned yet, so when Wrath stops, he lets me take back control, satisfied with the result. I reach my hand down and help him up. He gives me a nod.

"Thank you, Aridam."

"We good? You know it had to happen."

"Yeah, yeah, I know. We're good." He limps toward the kitchen, wanting to lick his wounds in private.

Drystan emerges, clapping Kek on the back hard enough that it was also a reprimand, before he addresses me. "Is Dev not showing?"

Devland's voice sounds from behind me. "No, I'm here. Let's get this over with. I'm so sorry, Aridam. What we did was unforgivable." He had just come in through the open sliding door. He must have caught Drystan's question.

He knows I won't go easy on him, so I don't mince words, just soundly beat him. I drop him once a blow knocks him out, leaving him in a heap until he comes back to. Drystan is still lounging in the room. It's only about a minute before Dev groans and sits up.

"I trusted you the most with my mate, Devland. You promised me. He was your responsibility." My voice cracks. Kek rejoined us while I was talking, so I address them both and hold nothing back.

"Wrath's punishment for you is done. We'll move on and be stronger for it. You do, however, need to do one more thing. My mate will not let you apologize; he doesn't hold you responsible. Belial and I do. To make it up to all of us, you will do a health check of Rhys's injuries tomorrow morning. I hate the thought of you setting eyes on my nearly naked mate, but you need to understand what your negligence caused. What succumbing to your sin's pull while you were in charge of a team member's mate's safety does. My mate *died* in my arms because of his injuries. I held him as our bond broke, as he took his last breath. Only the mercy of Michael and Rhys's own determination brought him back.

"His night terrors and screams will be mine to shoulder. The moments where he half wakes but doesn't see me, only sees his tormentor. When he screams and thrashes out of my arms in the middle of the night because I brushed against his wrists . . . all of that is my punishment. My mate suffered because I trusted someone else to protect him, and I put too much faith in his newly acquired accelerated healing. I am not without blame. We need to get past this as a team; we need to do better."

Devland's eyes are glassy, his pain evident. Kek avoids my gaze altogether, his shame radiating off him. I'll leave them to their thoughts.

"Team meeting tonight. You will attend. Now if you'll excuse me, I have to take my mate to see his friends."

- - -

"These chairs are tiny, Rhys." I look at the metal and faux wood contraption I'm sure was bought so as many people as possible could be jammed into the shop.

"Ooo, I don't think I like that." He frowns slightly.

"Like what?"

"You didn't even call me sweet, just Rhys. You never use just my first name unless you're stressed and I'm included in that stress. Makes me feel like I'm in trouble. Am I in trouble right now?"

"No!" I rush to reassure him. "I apologize, mate. I didn't realize I did that. I'll endeavor to only use nicknames from now on." That seems to satisfy him.

He sits at a small table, putting way too much faith in the construction of those chairs. He pats the one next to him, and I sit gingerly. The sides dig into my ass in the most unpleasant way. I grunt, hoping he's happy. "You can't even sit on my lap," I grouse.

He giggles. "It's only for an hour, big guy. You'll survive."

"Don't use that voice. I'm not a child."

"No, no, you are most definitely not." His salacious wink sends blood rushing to my dick. Now there's no way I can stand; my erection makes that impossible.

He notices and sighs dramatically. "I guess I'll go up and order so you don't scar some poor soccer mom or her kid." Humor laces his voice, so I know he's not too put out by it.

I watch him as he moves through the shop. I know he talked to Sasha about the change in his appearance, but he's nervous about how she'll react when she finally sees him in person. The video chat was hard to witness; tears covered my mate's face as he apologized to his best friend for keeping her in the dark. She still doesn't know about supernaturals, but she's aware that he was caught up in a classified mission. We let her believe the team is special ops and that secrecy is of the upmost importance if she wants to continue to see him. He hated lying to her but understood it was more for her own safety.

Rhys makes it back to the table when a beautiful red-haired woman in a long skirt enters the shop. She scans the patrons, and once I see her face, I can finally identify her as Sasha. Rhys's back is still to the door, so he doesn't see her expression as her eyes settle on him. It's pain and fear. He's wearing a plain grey wool scarf, which he says itches, but he doesn't want the stares. It works in his favor here since Sasha can't see the damage.

She makes her way over as he turns around, and they lock eyes. Her pace picks up to running, and she throws herself into my mate's arms. The hug is desperate and tight. Her sob is audible even with her mouth pressed against his shoulder. He pats her gently on the back, soothing her. I feel uncomfortable intruding on such a tender moment between friends, but moving would make it more awkward.

"I'm so sorry. I'm being so rude. Hello again, Ari." She holds out her hand while wiping her face with the other. Both Rhys and I crack a smile. She's just precious.

"Pleasure to meet you, Sasha; I've heard so much about you. Please, take a seat." I gesture to the seat across from Rhys and I, waiting for them to sit before pulling Rhys's legs into my lap.

Watching my mate sip his coffee and laugh is worth every minute in the godforsaken chair.

Around two hours and a thousand body adjustments later, I can tell Rhys is tiring.

"Hey, baby, if you wanted to still stop by the club, we should probably head that way."

"Oh! I didn't realize how long we've been here! Colin is probably waiting for me at the house. We'll do this again soon, okay, Rhysies?" She gives my mate a quick hug and a peck on the cheek, and then surprises me with the same. I have to practically bend in half to bring my cheek down to her. I can see Rhys's eyes crinkle at the corners as he covers his mouth to hide his laughter.

"Take care of him, okay?" Her voice is tinged with worry.

"Of course. Have fun today with Colin, Sasha." I turn to my mate. "Ready?"
 "Actually, can we just head home? I kind of want to rest. I didn't think it'd be so hard anymore."

"You're still recovering. Take all the naps you want." I kiss his temple as we head toward the alley behind the coffee shop. We portal home and walk into a bit of chaos.

"Belial, what's going on?"

"They have a witch! It explains everything! The different spells at every property, the illusions. Why didn't I see this before?! I need to get ahold of Az. He's in charge of rounding up the coven. Aridam, I might suggest getting him some backup. It's not a small job anymore."

Rhys sighs next to me, reminding me why we came home early.

"Of course, Bel. Just give me a few minutes." I go to walk him to our room, but his hand stays me.

"I can find the room myself, big guy. It's safe here. I'll go straight to the room to change and head to nap in Lily's room. She leaves tomorrow, so maybe she wants to watch a movie."

I'm torn, but I understand what he's saying. I have to loosen the reins a little. He hasn't been alone for more than a minute since he's been back. Wrath rumbles unhappily in my chest. He doesn't see the problem.

Chapter Seventeen

Rhys

I'm confused as to why I need an examination, especially by demons, when we've had Raphael of all people (angels?) take a look at me.

"Why, though, Ari? It doesn't make sense. I don't need them to look at me."

Ari's sigh is heavy. "We need them to see what happened, sweet Rhys. I know you don't want people to see you—I don't either—but this cannot happen again. What if we hadn't bonded yet? What if it's someone else's mate next time they decide to ignore Belial's orders over the comms? They have to really see. They weren't here when you told us your story; they heard it all second hand. Their punishment is to know they had a hand in what happened to you. You blame yourself, but you never should have been alone in the first place. When you left that room, Devland was supposed to have gone with you. Kek never should have passed you by; he should have stayed with you the second he saw you were alone in that hall. You've trained a few weeks, while we've trained our whole lives, baby. That's like allowing a freshman nursing student to do open heart surgery on that show you watch."

Mmm, McSteamy. "Ugh, I hate when you use logic. I don't like this, but I'll do it. You will not be in the room. I won't be able to concentrate, and if you scowl too long, I'll end up popping a boner."

A chuckle escapes him. "I'll be right outside the door."

Ari leaves me in the training room. We chose here instead of our room because we didn't want to make this any more intimate than it has to be. The door pushes open, and Devland slips through with Kek following close behind. They look awful, and my heart aches for them. I'm standing in my robe and briefs; otherwise, I would have rushed to hug them. I give them a big smile instead.

"So I get two sexy nurses today? How did I get so lucky?" My humor seems to break some of the tension, but their faces are still drawn. I don't want to let on that I know this is a punishment to them yet, if at all. The ruse gives us all an excuse to focus on not talking about it. I do owe them an apology, though . . . I shouldn't have run off on my own.

Kek speaks first, his voice rough. "Are you in pain anywhere?"

"Just a twinge occasionally." I know the worst is still covered, so I take a deep breath and double check with them. I won't force them to look at my damaged body no matter what Bel or Ari say. "Are you sure you want to see this? You don't have to. Raphael did an amazing job healing what he could."

I can practically see Devland's temptation to flee, his eyes shifting to the door. Kek, though, immediately shakes his head.

"No, Rhys. We need to see everything."

"Well, I won't be getting naked, mister, so you'll be missing the best bits, but it's your choice." I take a deep breath. "So . . . do I just take it off or would it be better to go section by section?"

I see their confusion, so I can assume the others told them nothing about the extent of my injuries. "Umm . . . it might be better to just rip off the Band-Aid." I quickly untie and pull off the robe, clenching it in my left fist away from my body. Devland makes a strangled sound, and his face crumples. Kek stays stock-still, eyes taking in my whole front. He pales when he looks at my neck and then turns a little green when he reaches my hip.

"Oh, Rhys, I'm so sorry." Devland's voice cracks.

"I'm sorry, too, guys. I shouldn't have left the hall. I overestimated how prepared I was for the supernatural world."

Kek still hasn't said anything, but he drifts closer, hovering his shaking hand over the missing piece of my hip.

"It's okay, Kek, I'm okay."

He just shakes his head. "Is this everything, Rhys?" A chill runs down my spine at the lethal calm that covers his face. He stares at my wrists and the permanent ligature marks covering them.

"Ummm . . . no." I rush to reassure him, though. "You don't have to look, Kek. This isn't your fault."

"Show us," Devland croaks.

I sigh and turn, revealing the giant brand and the bites covering my back. Paired gasps sound from behind me.

"Ari thinks a witch can remove or distort it. Hey, maybe I can just get tattoos and cover most of them."

"Fuck, Rhys. What did they do to you?! Oh God, I'm going to be sick."

I spin to see Devland rush from the room, his hand covering his mouth. My heart sinks. I knew this kind of reaction would happen, but it still hurts.

"It's not the sight of your injuries, Rhys. It's that we are responsible for them. You may not believe us, but we never wanted anything to happen to you. We will never forgive ourselves, and you shouldn't either."

I look into Kek's beautiful violet eyes and can't restrain myself anymore. I wrap my arms around his waist and squeeze him into a tight hug.

"Of course I forgive you. You're family." Kek's arms wrap around my shoulders in return, gently squeezing back.

"Let's go find your mate before he finds you hugging another man, wearing only underwear."

I jump back. Yeah, that'd be bad. I catch him wiping his eyes while I grab the robe I dropped a while ago. I slip it on, and we walk to the hall, not seeing Dev. Aridam waits patiently by the door, nodding to Kek as he passes and getting one in return.

He pulls me into his arms, hoisting me up so my legs wrap around his torso. He places a hand under my ass to support me and cups my face with the other. "I love you, sweet Rhys. Your reassurance is exactly what they needed."

"You heard all that?"

He chuckles, kissing my temple. "Yes."

"You know? Keeping secrets is going to be a bitch with you guys around."

"Good," he growls. "No secrets."

"I'm sorry to interrupt, but could I borrow your mate for a second, Aridam?" Bel's hesitant voice drifts over me. So much pain this little envy demon possesses.

"Of course." He kisses my nose and whispers his goodbyes, leaving me with Bel.

"Walk with me, Bel! I have to change back into some real clothes." He follows me quietly to my room, stopping just inside the door. I zip into the bathroom and throw on some sweats I finally found Lily hoarding in her room. I pause when grabbing my shirt.

"Bel?"

"Yeah?"

"Do you want to see me before I completely dress?"

His breath hitches so hard, I hear it through the door. "Yes, please, Rhys. I need to know. My imagination is killing me after Devland lost his lunch in the kitchen. I didn't want to ask, but if you're comfortable, I'd like to hug you too?"

Oh, sweet Bel. I walk out of the room, letting him analyze my front before showing him my back. After a few seconds, I turn back and see his tears falling once more.

"Oh, Bel-Bel. Come here." I wrap my arms around him. "You can't treat me like glass now, twinny. Hug me back!" He squeezes me until my ribs protest, crying into my shoulder.

"You shouldn't have to console me, Rhys. I should be your shoulder to cry on too."

"Nah, I'm done crying. After today, I'd like to stop feeling like an animal in the zoo, though. Could you just take some pictures for me so I can stop being half naked around my man's friends?"

He giggles softly and nods. He takes about ten minutes, getting all the angles. "Anything on your legs you want me to document?"

"Nope! Only cuts from my ass down, so no worries! If we can get someone to fix the scarring on a few of these bigger ones and the brand, I'd appreciate that. The cuts don't bother me as much as the bites." I shiver.

"Go ahead and put your shirt on, then, Rhys." I follow his direction and throw on my plain black T-shirt.

"I'm so glad you're okay, Rhys. Not just because you're my twin. You're such a good person. The world needs your light."

"Cheesy, just the way I like ya." I wink. "Wanna watch a movie and snuggle? We can use Lily's living room like we used to before. She won't mind."

"Please."

Once we're situated on the couch in the living room, I rest my head on his shoulder, letting him hug me to his side. I grab the blanket from the cushion beside me and cover us both. I'm drained. Exposing my vulnerability to the team today was hard. I don't regret it, exactly; I'm just worried they'll come to believe I'm a liability, and if I'm honest with myself, I am. I try to clear my mind and just *be*, drawing comfort from Belial.

Aridam

I find my mate in the living room, curled around Belial's sleeping form. They look so peaceful, I almost regret moving him. Almost. I gently shake Bel's shoulder, and he slowly blinks awake. We get him situated so I can lift my mate off the couch. He stirs a bit, rubbing his nose against my chest sleepily. So adorable.

"It's okay, sweet Rhys, go back to sleep."

"Mmmkay." His soft snores sound only a second after his mumbled reply. It's good to see my mate is actually sleeping without nightmares. By my estimate, it's probably been a few hours, more than he's gotten at once since he's been home.

I place him on our bed, covering him with a throw blanket. I grab my phone and check it for messages. A text from the realtor I contacted catches my eye. It includes links to homes in the area to my two polar opposite specifications. The first is a three-bedroom house, large windows, and a full backyard for entertaining. The next place, though, hits different. Twelve bedrooms, fourteen bathrooms, and every convenience you can imagine. I want to bring up moving up here with the team and need to have a price point reference. I have enough money to buy the house, but I don't want to waste the cash if it will break up the team's living situation or if no one wants it.

Now is as good a time as any. I shoot a message to Lily, asking if she'll sit with Rhys before she leaves. I hope she's still here, and I wait for her reply before getting up. A soft knock on the door sets me in motion. I kiss my mate's forehead before exiting the room, thanking Lily before portaling to the team house in Hell.

A deep breath exposes my nerves. I don't like not knowing where I stand with my team. I send a message in the group chat for the men to meet me here in twenty. I need to talk to the boss before I talk to the team, but I want this figured out today. Dialing Astaroth, I settle on the chair in my room. He picks up, and I rise to my feet again anyway, pacing.

"Good evening, Aridam. To what do I owe the pleasure?" His tone is deadpan, at odds with his words.

"Good evening, sir. I wanted to double-check on the living situation. It was irresponsible of me to put it off this long, and I want to rectify that. I assume we haven't found a way for Rhys to reside in Hell here at the team house?"

"I'm afraid not, Aridam. His soul, although not whole, is connected to his life. He's alive. He cannot enter The Three Gates or any place in Hell."

"Damn. I knew the chances were slim, but that puts us in an awkward position."

"How so? You move your team."

"I cannot simply command them to pack up their lives, sir."

He scoffs. "You most definitely can, though I understand why it would be better to have their cooperation. You can sell the current team house, pick another smaller one here in Hell, and have a large team house with your mate. The function of your team is the same. You are still my most trusted team in relation to the living world; you will not lose your positions unless your team proves unable to work cohesively any longer. I honestly don't care where you reside when you're not working, Aridam."

"Thank you, sir. It's a relief to have your support."
"So formal, Aridam. I assume your little mate isn't there to tease you?"

"No, sir, I'm at the team house, waiting for the guys. I've looked at properties in the New York City area and believe I've found one."

"Perfect! Would you like me to have Franco send you a list of available houses in the faction or would you like to build fresh?" I hear the rustling of papers and soft talking from his end.

"If he could send them, I'd appreciate it. We will move pretty quickly. I don't like not having the team consistently in one place."

"Done. It'll be to you in just a few. Good luck, Aridam. Update me when you've decided."

"Yes, sir." He hangs up. Fuck, I hope this works out how I'd like.

I make my way to the common area, noting everyone is gathered in the kitchen. I'm glad to see it. Belial being okay with the others shows he's been working hard at letting Rhys's incident go.

Only one person is missing, and it worries me. Azvameth needs to personally check in. I haven't seen him since before my mate's brush with death, and it's unacceptable. I text him before it slips my mind again. *Meeting is mandatory, Az.* No response.

"Bel?" He swings his gaze to me. "When was the last time you talked to Az?"

"Yesterday, why?"

"Can you call him, please?"

"Sure!" He walks away briskly, tapping the tech that always resides in his ear and pulling out his tablet.

"How is your mate, Aridam?" Devland still looks awful. His coloring has improved, but his tattoos have shifted repeatedly, meaning he's on the outs with his sin. I can't have him turning on himself like Drystan does.

"He's good, Dev, really good. I asked Lily to put some feelers out there for a witch who can help his scarring, so she's heading back to that coven out in the plains she went to before to ask around. Ohio, I think."

"Ah. Good. I'm sure you guys will think of something."

"Hey, Dev?" His miserable eyes swing up to meet mine. "Do you know one of the things they tempted him with during his appeal when he was gone?" A shake of his head. "They showed if he went to Reception like he should have, he would have been a greed demon. He understands you and your sin better than you think. He wholeheartedly believes you are his family now, and it hurts him that you avoid him. No, he hasn't said anything. I *feel* it, Dev. He wants his whole family happy and healthy . . . that includes you." His eyes fill with tears, and he nods, looking away to hide them falling.

Belial's voice comes from the doorway, startling Devland. "I hate to interrupt, but he's right, you know? I blamed you. Rhys never did. He loves us, so we need to get our heads out of our asses so we can make him happy, yeah?" Turning his head to me, he continues. "Azvameth will video conference in, but he can't be around the team right now. He has some shit going on. I won't spill secrets, but if he doesn't enlighten the team within a week, I'll tell you all myself." His warning glare to the phone shows he's not kidding at all.

"Alrighty then. Why don't you tell us why we're here, Oh Wrathful One?" Az's tone drips with sarcasm.

"Right. Okay." Deep breath. "My mate is human. Well, human-ish. He cannot step into Hell. So we need to make a few decisions as a team about where we will reside and how the new dynamics will work."

"Explain, please." Kieran looks worried. I know living around humans will be so hard for him. He and Belial are the ones I worry about the most with this plan.

"We have a few options." I explain the options Astaroth outlined for me, adding only one more. "We also have the option of splitting the team up. You do not have to follow me as your team lead. I know you could all find a new team within Astaroth's ranks. Hell, you'd get to have your pick."

"Shut up." Belial sounds a step beyond irritated. "No one is leaving the team. You were just preaching about family. Don't be a hypocrite. Now, we do have another option. We can build a new team house. I thought this issue might come up eventually, so I actually bought the land that Constantine's estate sat on. It's perfectly sized and far enough from neighbors that we don't have to worry about Kieran affecting the neighborhood. My issue is a little different, but I'm willing to work with whoever I need to in order to live with you guys at the team house like I do here. Maybe we can borrow the witch Astaroth used to leak-proof my room."

"Wow. Okay, I didn't even think of that. That's a great idea, Bel."

"I know." His smile this time is smug yet lighter. "I have one more thing I wanted to talk about before we move on this."

I make a motion for him to continue. He's hijacked my meeting, so I may as well sit back and enjoy the ride. "Rhys. He needs to become an official part of the team. I shot the proposal over to big boss man this morning and got the go-ahead to discuss with you all."

"Are you fucking nuts?!"

"Why would we put him in danger again?"

"Absolutely not!"

"No."

The shouting is loud, accusations flying wildly. Belial calmly puts up a hand to wait for us to stop yelling. Wrath slams against my skin, having already succeeded in changing forms.

"You all need a handler. I cannot keep doing it. My role in this team has become all-consuming. I sleep once a week for a few hours. Between handling all the tech, being liaison for every assignment, following up on old cases, researching current ones, the go between for you guys, even something as mundane as groceries for Lily's house. I currently have"—he looks at his tablet—"two hundred seventeen things on my list to get done in the next few days. So either we bring Rhys in to be our team PA, or we bring in another demon. You choose."

We fall silent. I feel guilty. I knew I was piling more and more onto Belial; I just didn't see how much.

"Shit, Belial, why didn't you say something?" Azvameth's voice comes from the tablet.

"I just did." His voice is dry, but his eyes flash with something like loneliness. He's been keeping extra busy because even on the team, he's alone most of the time. Fuck! That's it. When we first got together as a team, I noticed he went above and beyond to be as useful as possible. He still doesn't see himself as indispensable to us as a person, not just as the go-to guy on the team. I need to let Rhys know.

"I'll talk to him. We have a lot to discuss tonight. Lily needs to head out, so I'll end the meeting shortly. Everyone in favor of Rhys being the handler?" All hands rise, with an "aye" from Az on the tablet. "Everyone in favor of building a team house on the old vamp estate?" Five hands besides the one I didn't raise. It's the majority, but there are two who didn't. "Az? Kieran? What are your concerns?"

"I will go with what the team says, but I have another . . . concern . . . at the moment. I need to wrap up this assignment and then I'll update you all."

"Is it personal or does it affect the team?" I need to make sure.

"Both, but I won't start shit until I know what's going on. It'll be fine until then. I won't let it affect you guys."

"Fine. I believe Belial's warning was real. You have a week, Az. We're here if you need anything." He snorts but nods, ending the call. I turn to Kieran, waiting for his answer.

"I'm just nervous. Can we still keep a team house here? I don't want to not be able to come home and have a place to call my own." His voice is soft, more so than normal.

"Of course, Kieran. We will have a small team house here for recouping and visiting. I'm getting a list of current places from Franco today. Why don't I send you the list and you can help pick the place?" Kek's small smile lets me know I did the right thing by involving Kieran in the process.

"Okay. I want this wrapped up in the next few days. Let me know if we need to do anything further for the estate before I have blueprints drawn up." Bobbing heads meet my words. Perfect. "Thanks, guys." I waste no time portaling to my room at Lily's. I need to share the news with my mate.

Chapter Eighteen

Rhys

I love getting to spend some extra time with Lily. It feels like we've been friends for much longer than the few months that've passed. I've made some pretty decent friends here, if I do say so myself. She is the cool aunt or older cousin I always wanted.

"So, you're going to apply the cream every few hours for the next week. Don't forget, child. With you being mostly a Null, we need to start prepping your skin as much as possible so a spell will take. I'm hoping to find someone within a day or two. A witch with enough power won't be easy to find, let alone be willing to help after the Morozov coven fell, though. It was almost twenty years ago, but it still makes witches skittish."

"Got it. Have my mate rub me down multiple times a day. Oh, the hardship!" The last line was done in my best fainting woman voice; the "clutching my pearls" motion was the perfect dash of flare. We burst into giggles.

My chest warms, and I know my mate is once again happy. We had a minute of panic earlier, making me nervous. I knew from Lily that he had to get the team together to touch base, so why the panic? I know he can take care of himself; I just don't like being away from my hunk of man (demon?) meat for too long. My dick twitches at the thought that I may be able to convince my mate to wreck me later. He's been so gentle, and while I do love me some sweet lovin', sometimes I miss his rough treatment from before. I just need to push him to lose more control; maybe poking at Wrath a bit will help.

As if he could feel my arousal, my mate comes marching through the doors. He's a mix of horny and giddy. Ahh, perfect. "Ari! You're back!"

He leans down to kiss me gently. "Mhm. How was your visit, love?"

I am obsessed with his new nickname for me. Baby went straight to my dick, but this one does a little squeeze on my heart every time. I soften against him, begging for more kisses. His lips turn hard and demanding, and that is of course when Lily interrupts our moment with her trifling ass.

"I'll head out; did you guys need anything before I go?"

"I think we are okay, Lily, thank you. Please update Rhys or myself every day so we know what's going on and that you're safe. We took care of Constantine, but he wasn't the only player in the game."

"Understood, demon." Then to me, "Child."

It's a nickname I can stomach now without sassing back. It's definitely not my favorite, but I know she's not making fun of me anymore. I surprise her with a big hug.

Swiping the cream off the coffee table, I book it to our room, not waiting for Ari to catch up. He doesn't seem to mind my fast pace, but then again, his legs are a million miles long, so he's not even winded as he reaches me. I was practically jogging. I stop abruptly and spin, holding my arms up, not unlike a toddler. "Upsies, my magnificent steed!"

"I am not a horse."

"Steed . . . don't sass me. Get to steed-ing." I huff when he simply arches an eyebrow. "Ugh! Just take me to our room! I need you to rub some cream all over me. Unless you don't want to? I guess I could ask—Eeep!" I'm in his arms, clutching the jar so it doesn't fly out of my hands. He zooms the rest of the way to our room, placing me on the soft tan comforter while I'm still laughing.

He smiles all tender-like, and while I love that, I do, I want something a little more heated. I drop my hands to his pants, and his eyes darken immediately.

"I thought you needed me to rub you down with some of the witch's cream, sweet Rhys? We need *you* naked for that, not me."

"Please, big guy. I need you. More than I need food." His eyes start to swirl. Aha! Perfect. "I need my mate to show me I'm not glass. I need that demon D, big guy. Think you can help Ari out? He needs some nudging." I'm talking directly to Wrath, knowing he'll be pushing hard to either feed or fuck me. His demon form bursts out before I can ask again.

"Mate needs," he growls, and yanks me to him, jerkily divesting me of my clothes and running his hands over my scars. His forked tongue follows the path of his fingers, making me shiver. I need this, to get wrapped up in my mate. His tail wraps around my calf, a favorite spot.

"Lube, big guy." His swirling eyes slow but don't stop. I can feel their harmony click in through our bond. Their lust and longing rush into me, making me clench. His clawed hands fumble at the bedside table, eventually just ripping the drawer out. It clatters to the floor, and normally I would make a joke, but his fervor makes my breath catch.

While he's distracted with trying to find the bottle that must have rolled out of the drawer when it fell, I trail my fingers over his shoulders to his wings. I trace the designs starting at the tip, ending at spot where they merge with his skin, and he shivers. Sensitive, good. Bending my knees, I bring my legs up closer to me and stroke his tail with my free hand, enjoying the way it pulses and squeezes my calf in response. I commit the feeling of it to memory as best I can, slowly petting every inch I can reach. The heart-shaped barb gets special attention. It has been in my mouth . . . so, ya know, I want to make sure it knows I like it. Ari told me it kind of has a mind of its own, so I want to coax it into playing with me. I wonder what it would feel like to be fucked by his tail. Like in reverse from what we've done before?

My demon must catch on to my train of thought, because his head swings my way, the lube in his grasp. His black hair falls artfully, framing his face. His smile is smug, wicked. His fangs poke over his bottom lip just a tad, calling to me. His tail unwinds, releasing itself from my grip. It skates across my skin and leaves goosebumps in its wake. My entire lower body fills with heat as it teases the fleshy underside of my ass, wiggling its way into my crease. I gasp, feeling it brushing lightly over my hole.

The light touch paired with Ari's otherwise vise-like grip is intoxicating. He watches my face so intently, and I'm sucked into his silver eyes. I've seen his tail in all its glory, and it's big, but since Ari has been using his fingers on me often enough, I know I can take his tail with little prep. The girth of his barb is about three fingers thick, definitely not as wide as his ridged monster but enough to wreck me . . . and so, so long. It could probably poke my belly button from the inside.

"You wanna feel me inside you, sweet Rhys? Have my tail open you up? Get you ready for my cock? Let's see how many times I can make you come tonight, baby. You asked for this, so you'll take it like such a good boy."

I moan as my response. I did ask for this. It's perfect. His tail surprises me by being wet. I don't know when he applied lube, but I'm glad he did as he gently pushes and strokes my tight ring. The skin softens under his ministrations, allowing the pointed tip to slip in. The barb is the size of an average/large plug, so it's sucked into me with some strained effort on my part since we didn't stretch me out. We groan in unison as I clench down, his barb having popped all the way in. It slithers in further, slowly torturing my insides. So full.

He doesn't wait long before he starts shallowly thrusting his tail. His cock rubs against mine, the ridges massaging the underside of my shaft. I can already see stars. His clawed fingers make their way to my nipple, pinching lightly. "Such a good mate, look at you. So pretty, bouncing back on my tail. Wanna see you come like this. Need to feel your ass milk my tail with your orgasm. So sweet." His tail rubs against my prostate while his barb seems to be poking my throat somehow. I can feel my orgasm starting, the tingle in my gut twisting. He grabs both our dicks with a large hand, careful of his claws, and starts stroking us together. He's thrusting his tail and cock at the same time, overloading me with pleasure.

I writhe on the bed, trying to meet his thrusts and pull away from the overload of sensation at the same time. Even my dick is confused. I'm so turned on it hurts. My fists clench the sheets and my head slams back onto the mattress. "So close! Please, please! Ari!" I need relief or I'll die. He rumbles low in his chest. He pinches my nipple hard enough to draw blood, and it's enough to tip me over. My orgasm finally explodes through my body, my mind going blank. I can't breathe as I shoot all over our cocks and my chest. He keeps stroking, using my release as lube before adding his own load. His neck is taut, veins protruding. He's violently beautiful, even during orgasm. He gives a final grunt, and his hips finally falter, his tail spasming inside me. Still twitching, my own body gives out.

"I'm not done with you yet, mate." His growled promise sends another spurt of come out of me.

"Promises, promises," I weakly tease.

He rolls us onto our sides and proceeds to prove he's a man of his word, fucking me until I pass out.

- - -

Ari is still inside me when I wake up. It's a feeling I could easily become addicted to. I know he's awake. His large clawless hand caresses my stomach, which is a little bloated with how many orgasms he's keeping in there. I feel whole and full, so I just soak up the attention.

"You distracted me, love. I had news I wanted to share, and I was supposed to apply your cream."

"Are you complaining?"
A chuckle vibrates his chest against my back. "Absolutely not. I just thought you'd like to know what we decided on as a team, and how it affects you." That sounds ominous. I wiggle to turn around, ignoring the empty feeling he leaves behind as he slips from my body.

"Is everything okay? Did I do something?"

He kisses my nose. "Of course not, my mate. We actually have a proposal for you." He reaches over to where I'd dropped the cream earlier and unscrews the cap.

"What kind of proposal? I don't like the suspense! Just tell me!" He may feel the tendril of anxiety running through me, so he relents, starting to rub in the smelly-ass lotion while he talks.

"We want to bring you in as part of the team." He places a finger not covered in cream over my lips to stem the flow of questions he's aware will spill out any second. My mind races, but I wait for him to finish. "It's been brought to my attention that Belial is being extremely overworked. He's actually the one who came up with the idea that we need a handler. You would stay back at base during assignments, but you'd be responsible for a lot, and I do mean A LOT of behind-the-scene things. Belial will

continue to run tech and research for our team, but you would be a coordinator. What do you think?" He stalls a second to brace himself before he removes his finger, dipping his other hand in the jar to continue his task.
 "Did the whole team say they wanted me, or did you just decide?" His clean finger is back.

"The whole team. We voted and it was unanimous, love." Finger removed. More rubbing.

"What does the position entail?" I shut my own trap and get a kiss as a reward, and no finger. I'm such a good boy.

"You'll have to train with Belial for a while so he can explain everything. I know nothing other than you have to be quick on your feet."

"I can problem solve like a motherfucker, just you wait. I'll make this job my bitch."

A laugh bursts from him, and I memorize the unfettered, surprised joy on his face. "I have no doubt. The only thing left now is to build our home base. We are moving up here as a team, but we'll keep a small house in Hell for a backup." He's done with my torso and arms, so he gently turns me over to start on my back.

"That's awesome! Do you know where you're building?"

"We."

"Sorry, do you know where you guys are building?" I stare at the wall of the bland room, waiting for the answer. I hope it's close.

"No, baby. Us. You and me. *We* are building the team house. It'll be your home too, so you get to help me make all the decisions."

My eyes tear up. I don't wait for him to finish with my back. I need to face him. "It'll be our home? Like a permanent home?" He looks confused. "I've never had a place to really call my own before. I've had an apartment to myself for a couple weeks, but I rented, and it was in a shitty area I never would have stayed in. Y-you really want to b-build a forever home with m-me?" My tears are flowing, and I'm a snotty mess at this point, hiccupping and stuttering through my words.

"Shh, baby, of course I do. You're everything to me." His arm squeezes tighter, cradling my head into his neck. His clean hand rubs soothing circles on my back, trailing over my ass. His lust thrums through the bond, distracting me.

"You're horny right now?"

"I'm always horny around you, but yes. Your eyes are so glassy and vulnerable, your body pliant and shaking. I want to comfort you, but another part of me is envisioning your tear-streaked face stuffed with my cock."

His words light me on fire. I now desperately need to fulfill that vision. I need the comfort of my mate's body. I slither down as he loosens his arms, sucking marks into his skin. I give small bites, knowing how much he enjoys it. "Want all of you."

"You sure, love?"

"Please, mate."

His body switches again, the red hue so alluring. I've asked him why he seems to default to human, and his honest answer was that he was used to it; it didn't hurt to be in one form more than the other. I love his body both ways, but there's something special about seeing him as he truly is that gets me going. I'm going to spend the rest of my life worshiping this man, and I can't wait.

Epilogue

Rhys

Three Weeks Later

"Wait up, mister!" I call out to Azvameth as he darts out of the room. He's been impossible to pin down lately. I know he and Ari had this giant "come to Lucifer" moment about two weeks ago, but I don't know details. It's not fair that he knows things I don't. I've pulled out every trick I know to get him to cave, but it's like he's a vault of secrets. Hypocrite man.

"You'll catch him one day." Kek's patronizing tone doesn't rub me the wrong way anymore; I've gotten to know him better since I've officially joined the team. The interview I insisted on having with Astaroth before I came on as a paid member was terrifying, but he told Ari I was a "breath of fresh air." Damn right I was! I couldn't tell you why he thought that, though. I laughed at my own jokes and almost pissed myself when he got growly after I told him the system they had set up for paying the bills up here for his demons was stupid. Apparently it was his system. I tried to make him feel better by assuring him that a hundred years ago it was probably the best they had. I got nervous and snarked way too hard, but he laughed instead of beheading me, so win-win.

"Shut up. Where is your report on the alpha that disappeared? You said you'd have it to me three days ago, pride-alicious. Chop chop." His parting scowl is the best thing about this day so far.

I'm late to two different meetings, and I still can't track down my mate. I hope he feels all my frustration right now. I whip out my phone and dial him again. He actually answers this time. "Hello, love."

"Don't you 'hello, love' me, dick eater! Why am I still here? Don't we have to meet the builders at one?"

"Nope, I got that pushed back to one thirty."

"And the—"

"The call with Lily is in just a few minutes. I'll be to you in just a second. I had to find a place to portal home with all these boxes of cake mix. What are we doing with these again?"

"We're baking Belial a giant birthday cake, Mr. Interrupter. Hurry up." I end the call and wait, knowing my mate hates when I hang up without saying I love you. It'll hopefully earn me a spanking. I giggle to myself as Ari shows up with his signature scowl and arms loaded full of grocery bags.

"Belial won't eat all this, love."

"No, but Drystan might, and I want him to be able to pig out if he wants. We need to keep him healthy." He sighs but bows to my logic, placing all the bags in the kitchen.

My phone rings as he puts up the last of the funfetti boxes. I scramble to answer. "Lily! How goes it?" Her face looks tired and there's no smile in sight, so I know it's probably not good news.

"Are you both there?"

Ari pops his head into the frame, picking me up and settling me on his lap on the couch. "Yep, we're both here." My voice is fake cheery, but she seems too tired to notice, which is the point.

"I've asked everyone, Rhys. I'm so sorry, but I can't track down who helped Constantine. There's no witch who can match their power that I know of who's still alive, so I don't know what to do."

"Take a break, come home, and rest. Recuperate. We shouldn't have asked you to be out there that long." Ari's statement isn't pointed at me, but I still feel guilty.

"It's okay, Lily. I, uh . . . I . . . I don't need to find anyone. We've tried. I'll put finding a solution on the back burner for now. I know we could just remove the skin altogether. We'll find a good time and just be done with it. I can deal with how it looks, but the look on Kek's and Dev's faces every time we train with shirts off guts me. The team still beats themselves up for it, and I just want to move on."

"Are you sure?" Her voice is equal parts hopeful and sad.

"Yes, Lil. Thank you for trying as hard as you did." A sound distracts me for a second. I swear I heard footsteps, but who would still be here? Everyone else is at the team house packing, except Kek and Az, and they're both avoiding me. Ari remains passive, so I assume whatever it was wasn't a threat.

"Want me to portal you back?" Ari's offer is genuine.

"No. I want to bring my new RV back too, demon, and that's a little too much even for you."

"Fair. So we'll see you soon?" I ask.

"A few days at most, child. Talk later." She hangs up.

I allow myself to finally feel the disappointment running through me right now. All that time spent looking, and nothing. I blink away tears. No. I'm not a weak-ass bitch. I'll be fine.

"I love you, sweet Rhys."

"Scars and all?"

"Scars and all."

"I love you, too, big guy." I move to stand, holding out my hand like this goliath of a man needs my help standing. He takes it anyway and kisses it as he pulls himself off the couch.

"Let's go design a house a Hilton would kill for." I wink at him and soak up the sound of his gruff chuckle. Yeah, we'll be just fine.

AUTHOR'S NOTE

Thank you so much for reading *His Wrath*! I hope you enjoyed it and fell in love with the guys as much as I did. Please leave a rating and review so others can too!

WANT MORE?!

This will be part of an 8-book series following our favorite team of demons.

Next up? Azvameth getting in way over his head. His story will be told in *His Sloth*.

Xoxo,

Ava